# Twisted Beautiee 2
## An Erotic Thriller

# Twisted Beautiee 2
## An Erotic Thriller

BY

**TRACY WILSON**

http://beautifulpublications.com

Published by
Beautiful Publications LLC
Stratford, CT 06614

**PRINT ISBN: 978-0-9985765-7-2**
**EBOOK ISBN: 978-1-7331792-6-3**

Printed in the United States of America

## Dedication

I dedicate this series to my alter ego, Beautiee.

# Chapter 1

"Good morning," Sam said as we walked into work...

"Good morning," Bazil said as he headed towards our office...

"Good morning Sam – is Joselyn in yet?" I asked...

"She's in her office – you need me to get her for you?"

"No thanks – I'll go get her in a minute..." I said as I went down the hall towards our office... "Excuse me... Mr. Osgood?" I asked as I closed the door behind me and locked it...

"Yes... Mrs. Osgood?" Bazil asked as I walked towards him...

"Well..." I said as I started kissing him... "I've... always... had... this... fantasy..."

"Mmmmmm... tell me..."

"I've always... dreamed... that... one day..."

"Go on..." Bazil said as he began kissing me on my neck..."

"Oooohhh...."

"You were saying..." Bazil breathed as he continued kissing me on my neck and in between my breasts...

"One day... my boss... would fuck me... on his desk..."

"Your wish..." he said as he slid my shirt off my shoulders... "Is my command..." he breathed as he took my breasts out of my bra and began alternating between sucking my left nipple and then the right...

"Bazil..." I whispered as he pushed me down onto the desk and slid up my skirt...

"Ssshhh...." Bazil whispered as he opened my legs, slid my panties to the side, and slid himself inside me...

"Bazil..." I moaned as he laid himself on top of me and began thrusting...

"Ssshhh..." he moaned in my ear as he began thrusting deeper...

"I can't help it... fuck!" I moaned... Bazil covered my mouth with his to muffle my moans while picking up the pace as I grabbed his ass, pushing him in deeper... "MmmmMmmm... MmmmMmmm... MmmmMmmm..."

"Mmmmmph! Mmmmmph! Mmmmmph!"

"MmmmMmmm! MmmmMmmm! MmmmMmmm!"

"Mmmmmph! Mmmmmph! Mmmmmph!"

"Mr. Osgood... that was... so... fucking good..." I breathed between kisses....

"It... was... my... pleasure... Mrs. Osgood..."

"Mrs. Osgood?" Joselyn yelled as she knocked...

"Yes Joselyn?" I answered as Bazil and I jumped up off the desk and quickly adjusted ourselves...

"May I come in?"

"Yes Joselyn – just a sec," I said as I hurried to the door, unlocked it, and opened it...

"What's wrong Joselyn?" Bazil asked when he saw her face...

"Ummmmm... I have your mail..." she said with her head down...

"Joselyn... do I need to get Sam?" Bazil asked...

"Ummmmm... yea... let's get Sam..."

"Sam?" I called out...

"Yes Mrs. Osgood?" Sam answered as he came into the office... "Babe... what's wrong?" Sam asked when he saw Joselyn...

"I'm okay... but... they may not be..." she answered as she gave Sam an envelope...

"Oh shit!" Sam yelled...

"What is it?" Bazil asked...

"Here..." Sam said as he gave Bazil the envelope. Bazil opened the envelope... and bust out laughing...

"Bhaaaa..... haaa..... haaa....." Bazil laughed as he read the letter and then handed it to me to read...

"Bhaaaa..... haaa..... haaa....." I laughed as I read it...

"Damn... y'all are taking this real well!" Joselyn laughed...

"Oh I'm mad as hell right now Joselyn – but that's not why I'm laughing..."

"Well... what's so funny?" Joselyn asked...

"Well Joselyn..." I laughed... "If MaryJane had stayed in her place – she'd be fine – but since she seems to think she can threaten me and then turn around and demand we pay her unemployment – they're going to find out she ain't nothin' but a hoe!" I laughed again...

"You can't call her a hoe Mrs. Osgood..." Sam said...

"Joselyn – lets go to your office – I was coming to see you later today anyway..." I said as I walked out of our office, completely ignoring what Sam said...

"Bazil – she can't call MaryJane a hoe – she'll open us up to a lawsuit," Sam said.

"Sam... Beautiee won't do anything to hurt us – but whatever she does – that Bitch won't get unemployment..."

"What if MaryJane contests it?"

"What if she does?"

"Are you sure we don't have anything to worry about?"

"I'll call Smalls... just in case..."

"Okay... good... I'll see you later..." Sam said as he left the office...

"Attorney Smalls office – how may I assist you?" the receptionist answered...

"Good morning – it's Mr. Osgood – may I speak with Smalls?"

"Yes Sir Mr. Osgood – hold please...

"Yes Bazil," Smalls answered...

"Good morning to you too..." Bazil laughed.

"Good morning Bazil – what's up?"

"I have a situation with an employee..."

"Are you being sued for sexual harassment?"

"Not yet..."

"Bazil! What the fuck man!"

"I didn't..."

"Bazil – don't bullshit me!"

"I'm not..."

"Why'd you call me then?"

"She was fired..."

"Was she fired because she said no?"

"Smalls... you know me better than that..."

"I'm sorry Bazil – I have to ask..."

"I was fuckin' her though..."

"See! I knew it!"

"It wasn't like that..."

"Sigh... What happened Bazil?"

"She threatened my wife... she had to go..."

"Okay – she threatened your wife – wait a minute – you got married?"

"Yes."

"When?"

"Last Sunday."

"Congratulations."

"Thank you."

5

"So she threatened your wife?"

"Yes."

"Where?"

"In the ladies room."

"Were there any witnesses?"

"Yes."

"Hmmmmm... okay — so what's the problem?"

"She filed for unemployment."

"Oh... I see..." Smalls laughed.

"What's so funny?"

"She thought she was gonna keep gettin' the dick but you got married on her ass!" Smalls laughed.

"I love you man..." Bazil laughed.

"I love you too — you shouldn't have a problem — your wife has witnesses so even if she contests it you should be fine — in the meantime — if she calls you make sure your conversations are recorded..."

"Thank you Smalls..."

"You're welcome Bazil — I gotta take this call — keep me posted..." Smalls said as he hung up...

"Sam?" Bazil said as Sam answered his phone...

"Yes Bazil?"

"I need you to pick up a Bluetooth Cell Phone Recorder from the Spy Centre..."

"Yes Sir!" Sam said as he hung up the phone and left the office...

"Joselyn, did the notice come with a form for us to fill out?" I asked...

"Yes Mrs. Osgood – here," Joselyn said as she handed it to me and I read it...

"Haa haa! Let's go! Joselyn – take this down!"

"Yes Mrs. Osgood – go 'head..."

"Reporting Facts: Social Security Number."

"I'll fill that in – next..."

"Claimant Title: Bitch, Hoe!"

"Personal Assistant!" Joselyn laughed...

"Rate of Pay: Too Much!" I laughed...

"I can't wichu Mrs. Osgood..." Joselyn laughed...

"Last Day Physically Worked: Still Hoeing – last day here – January 20, 2019!" I laughed...

"Stop it!" Joselyn laughed...

"Length of Employment: Too long!"

"I agree!" Joselyn laughed...

"Date of Separation (if different than the last date physically worked): Same day I let go of her hair – after I dragged her ass!"

"Mrs. Osgood..." Joselyn laughed... "I'ma need you to stop... okay?"

"Name of Immediate Supervisor:" I just rolled my eyes...

"I got it – next..." Joselyn laughed...

"Reason for Separation: Misconduct/Fired"

"Oh definitely – next..."

"Who terminated the claimant?"

"Beautiee Osgood!" Joselyn laughed...

"Person's Job Title:"

7

"Same as your husband... right?"

"Yes Joselyn..."

"Okay – next"

"Provide a brief incident of the final incident that resulted in the claimant's separation: While in the ladies room, MaryJane LaRue told Joselyn Logan, another employee, she'd been here too long for a Bitch to think she could knock her out of her position..."

"Sure did!" Joselyn acknowledged as she continued taking notes...

"This conversation was witnessed by Sheila Henley, CFO."

"Sure was – I'll get this out right away..." Joselyn said as she went to get up...

"I'm not done Joselyn..."

"There's more?"

"Yes..."

"Okay – go 'head..."

"Shortly after leaving the ladies room, she went to my husband's office, told him she would put his dick in her mouth, and attempted to unbuckle his pants..."

"What?! Oh hell no – I'da been in jail if that was Sam!" Joselyn yelled...

"I should be in jail too... but I'm not..." I laughed.

"Did my mother hear that?"

"No she didn't... but your mother saw me drag that ass!" I laughed...

"Mrs. Osgood?"

"Yes Joselyn?"

"I know she's a hoe... but..."

"Yes Joselyn?"

"Do you really want me to put that in there?"

"Joselyn... as my mother would say... Ain't that what I said?"

"Yes Mrs. Osgood..." Joselyn laughed... "I'll get this out right away – Mrs. Osgood?"

"Yes Joselyn?"

"Are you signing the form?"

"This is my husband's company – run it by him and if he's okay with it, have him sign it..."

"Yes Mrs. Osgood," Joselyn said as she got up...

"Meet me in the cafeteria when you're done – I like the way you make coffee..." I said as I headed towards the cafeteria. When I got in the cafeteria I picked a table near the window and sat down to wait for Joselyn...

"Girl – did you see how his wife threw her down then had the nerve to tell her to get the fuck up and get the fuck out?" a young lady laughed...

"She betta then me – I would'a turned around and whooped her fuckin' ass!" another young lady laughed...

"Girl you would'na done shit but get the fuck out like his wife said..." the first young lady laughed...

"Well... I know you don't like her... but that's still my friend," the second young lady said...

"Well... your friend fucked herself out of a job..." the first young lady laughed...

"You just mad 'cause she didn't like you!" the second young lady laughed...

"Girl please – I don't need a bitch to like me – I have plenty of friends..." the first young lady laughed...

"Well I'ma still be her friend – there's two sides to a story ya know - oh hey Joselyn..."

"Hey Cheryl, hey Tracy... here's your coffee Mrs. Osgood..."

"Good morning ladies..." I said as I turned around to face them...

"Oh my God – Mrs. Osgood – please don't fire me – I'm sorry! Cheryl pleaded...

"Sorry you're friends with MaryJane... or sorry you can't beat my ass?" I continued drinking my coffee as Joselyn, Tracy, and Cheryl looked at me with their mouths open... "Well... what exactly are you sorry for?" I asked as I finished my coffee. Joselyn sat there drinking her coffee, smiling with glee at the 'tea'...

"I'm sorry Mrs. Osgood – it won't happen again..." Cheryl said with her head down...

"Tracy?"

"Yes Mrs. Osgood?"

"Who do you report to?"

"I report to Mrs. Henley..." she answered nervously...

"And who do you report to Cheryl?"

"I work in payroll..." she answered with her head down...

"You can go now ladies..."

"Yes Mrs. Osgood..." they said in unison as they left the cafeteria...

"What the hell is goin' on?" Joselyn asked...

"They were having a conversation... they had no idea I was sitting here..." I laughed...

"Did she really say she would'a beat your ass?"

"She did..." I laughed.

"You ain't mad?"

"Naa... I used to talk shit behind my bosses back too... I just never got caught!" I laughed...

"I'm learning more about you every day..." Joselyn laughed...

"Well I sure hope you like what you're learning..." I laughed...

"I sure do!" Joselyn laughed...

"Good morning Mrs. Osgood..." Sheila said as she sat down at the table with us...

"Good morning Sheila..." I said...

"Is everything okay?"

"Everything's fine... why do you ask?"

"Well... I was talking to Tracy... and she said you might have a problem..."

"I'm actually having a great day... so far... thanks for checking on me though... are you done with your coffee Joselyn?"

"Yes Mrs. Osgood..." Joselyn answered...

"Good – we need to get back to work – I'll be with my husband – come see me there..." I said as I got up and made a beeline towards Sheila's office. I didn't have to go too far because I ran into Tracy on my way to the ladies room...

"Oh hi Mrs. Osgood..."

"I was on my way to see you..."

"Is something wrong Mrs. Osgood?"

"Yes Tracy..."

"What did I do?"

"Don't insult my intelligence Tracy – you know exactly what you did..."

"All I said was..."

"Tracy?" I interrupted... "Don't make a problem where a problem doesn't exist – okay?"

"Yes Mrs. Osgood..."

"Which way is Payroll?"

"To the left at the end of the hall..."

"Thank you Tracy..." I said as I headed to Payroll... "Good morning everyone..." I said as I entered the area...

"Good morning Mrs. Osgood..." Cheryl said as she approached me... "Can I help you with anything?"

"As a matter of fact, you can – I was coming to see you..."

"Yyyou were?" she asked nervously...

"Yes – I need MaryJane LaRue's payroll records – could you get those for me?"

"Yes Mrs. Osgood – right away!"

"Thank you Cheryl – bring them to our office as soon as you have them..." I said as I headed back to see Bazil...

"Okay Mrs. Osgood..." When I got to the office Bazil got up from the desk, came towards me, pulled me into his arms, and kissed me passionately...

"Mmmmmm..... Beautiee..."

"Wow..." I breathed... "What did I do to deserve that?"

"You married me..." he said as he pulled me into another kiss...

"Oh – excuse me – Mrs. Osgood?"

"Yes Cheryl?"

"Here's the payroll records for MaryJane LaRue you asked for..." she said as she placed the folder on the desk and turned to leave the office...

"Cheryl?"

"Yes Mr. Osgood?"

"Was MaryJane paid everything she was owed when she was terminated?"

"She was paid everything except her overtime," Cheryl answered...

"Why wasn't she paid for her overtime?"

"Overtime has to be approved... and we couldn't pay it until you signed off on it..."

"Why wasn't it brought to my attention?"

"Mrs. Osgood ordered her off the premises..."

"Cheryl?" Bazil asked as he picked up the file and started going through it...

"Yes Mr. Osgood?"

"I need you to get this processed asap..." Bazil instructed as he signed the overtime request and gave it to her along with the folder...

"Yes Mr. Osgood – is there anything else?"

"Not at the moment..."

"Thank you Mr. Osgood..." Cheryl said on her way out...

"Beautiee..."

"Yes Mr. Osgood?" I answered seductively...

"We need to talk...

"We do?" I asked with concern in my voice...

"Yes Beautiee... come here..." he said as he held me...

"What's wrong Bazil?" I asked as I looked up at him...

"I had to make a change to the Notice of Unemployment Claim..."

"Bazil – you better not be telling me you gave that Bitch unemployment!"

"Hell no – but I had to make a change..."

"Okay..."

"I took out the part about... you know..."

"I knew you were going to do that..."

"She could sue for sexual harassment – and she could claim that I forced her..."

"Did you?"

"Beautiee... how could you ask me that?"

"Did you?"

"No Beautiee..."

"Okay then..."

"I called our attorney..."

"Why would you need to call your attorney if you didn't do anything?"

"Because I did something Beautiee..."

"Oh God Bazil..."

"It was consensual..."

"Oh thank God..." I breathed...

"Sam suggested I call Attorney Smalls just in case..."

"Does he know?"

"Yea... he knows..."

"Excuse me – Mrs. Osgood?"

"Yes Joselyn?"

"I need y'all to come with me..."

"Is everything okay?" Bazil asked...

"I need y'all to come with me..." Joselyn repeated...

"Okay... we're coming..." I said as we followed Joselyn to the lobby...

"Surprise!" everyone yelled...

"Oh my God, oh my God, oh my God!" I screamed as I jumped up and down and ran to hug David Bromstad from HGTV...

"I guess you know who I am..." David laughed as he hugged me back...

"Bazil... did you know about this?" I asked...

"I had no idea – I'm Bazil Osgood," Bazil said as he extended his hand to shake David's hand...

"I'm David Bromstad from Colorspash on HGTV," David beamed as he shook Bazil's hand and the cameras filmed us live...

"Oooohhh look... its David Bromstad!" a few of the employees shouted as they came running towards the lobby...

"We're here today because we received a letter from one of your employees..." David said as Bazil and I started looking around... "Is there a Joselyn Logan here?" David asked...

"I'm Joselyn!" Joselyn beamed as she went towards David and gave him a hug...

"Joselyn wrote us a letter explaining that you were looking to have your office re-decorated and that you specifically wanted light, bright and airy colors," David beamed as he wrapped his arm around Joselyn before continuing... "Joselyn also told us you're newlyweds," David said...

"Yes we are..." Bazil answered, pulling me close to him...

"I love love, romance, and weddings – so when we received this letter from Joselyn – I told the producers we have to do this and the producers agreed – it's our wedding gift to you," David beamed.

"Oh my Goooddddd!" I screamed as I jumped up and down... "Thank you, thank you, thank you!"

"You're welcome – we need to wrap this up so what I'd like to do is go to your office, discuss options, and show you what I've come up with..." David said as the crew members came closer...

"Our office is down the hall here…" Bazil said as we went down the hall to the office. Once we got inside David began to do what he does best…

"I understand you want to expand and you want this wall down – is that correct?"

"Yes it is," I beamed.

"Mr. Osgood – is there anything that's off limits?" David asked…

"As long as I'm not walking into a women's lounge, I'm fine…" Bazil laughed…

"I understand – now I have a few ideas I'd like to show you…" David said as he took out his drawings…

"Oh wow – these are nice!" Bazil said as he looked at them… "Beautiee – what do you think?" he asked as he handed the drawings to me…

"I like them all… but this one stands out…" I said pointing to the $3^{rd}$ drawing…

"I was hoping you'd pick that one – it's actually my favorite…" David gushed…

"We'll go with that one then…" Bazil said as he pulled me close to him…

"I can't wait to get started – we'll get that wall down first thing – once we do that, your new office will be done in about a week…" David said.

"That soon?" Bazil asked…

"Oh yea – by the way – is there another office you can use in the meantime?" David asked…

"You can use my office…" Joselyn volunteered…

"Thank you Joselyn – but where will you go?" I asked...

"I'll go in the office with my husband until your office is ready..." Joselyn answered.

"Thank you Joselyn..." I said as I hugged her...

"You're welcome Mrs. Osgood..."

"Hey everyone – what's going on?" Sam asked as he walked in...

"We're going to be on HGTV..." Bazil answered...

"Oh wow – how'd that happen?"

"Your wife wrote them a letter and told them we were newlyweds, so David Bromstad is designing our new office as a wedding gift to us..."

"Babe... you did?" Sam asked...

"I did..." Joselyn beamed...

"How'd I get such an awesome wife?" Sam asked as he pulled Joselyn into a kiss..."

"You prayed for me..." Joselyn answered as the cameras continued filming...

# Chapter 2

Sam waited for David Bromstad and everyone else from HGTV to leave for the day before he approached Bazil...

"Here..." Sam said as he handed Bazil the Bluetooth Cell Phone Recorder...

"Thank you Sam..." Bazil said after looking in the bag...

"Do you need any help setting this up?"

"Nope..."

"Good thing you asked me to get this for you — I don't trust her..."

"Neither do I Sam..." Bazil said as he took everything out the bag, opened it, and connected it to his cell phone as instructed..."

"I'm going to take my wife to lunch..." Sam said as he turned to leave Bazil in the office...

"Okay Sam... I'll see you later..." Bazil said as he hooked up the recorder... "I knew it wouldn't be long..." Bazil said out loud as he received a call from a private number... "Okay..." Bazil said out loud as he answered the call using the recorder...

"Hello Bazil..."

"MaryJane... what can I do for you?"

"You wanna play with me muthafucka?"

"I'm no longer interested in playing with you ever again..."

"You fucked with the wrong Bitch Bazil!"

"I sure did..."

"Did you get my gift?"

"Are you referring to your Notice of Unemployment Claim?"

"You know exactly what the fuck I'm referring to Bazil... and you better pay me..."

"I'm not paying you MaryJane..."

"Keep playing with me Bazil..."

"As I said... I'm no longer interested in playing with you ever again..."

"I'll tell them you raped me... and they'll believe me..."

"I was hoping you wouldn't threaten me...You and I both know I never raped you..."

"I'm just getting started muthafucka..."

"MaryJane... it's over... I'm married now... the only woman I want to play with is my wife..."

"Bazil... don't make me come for you..."

"Are you threatening me like you threatened my wife?"

"I never threatened your wife Bazil..."

"Are you calling my wife a liar?"

"I never threatened your wife..."

"So... are you calling Joselyn a liar?"

"That fuckin' Bitch!"

"So you did threaten my wife..."

"Bazil... I didn't mean it like that... I swear..."

"It doesn't matter MaryJane... it's over... you'll be paid your overtime... then I hope to never hear from you or see you ever again..."

"You forget... I know where all the bodies are buried... I can lead the cops to the graves..."

"Oh yes... now I remember... so how is your novel coming along?"

"So this is it? This is how you're gonna do me? After all I did for you?"

"MaryJane - all you did for me was give me pussy and suck my dick... everything else you did was for you..."

"What the fuck is that supposed to mean?"

"You were hired as my personal assistant and you were paid well... even though you came in when you wanted to and left early whenever you felt like it..."

"You never had a problem with that..."

"As I said... you gave me pussy and you sucked my dick..."

"If you don't pay me my unemployment... you're going to regret it..."

"MaryJane?"

"Yes Bazil?"

"Lose this number!" Bazil said as he disconnected the call, placed the recorder in his pocket, and came to Joselyn's office...

"Hello Mr. Osgood," Joselyn said as Bazil came into the office...

"Hello Joselyn – I need to speak to my wife... in private..." he said as he gave Joselyn a wink...

"That's okay – I can get the rest of my things later – Sam's taking me to lunch so I'll be back later..." she said as she left. Bazil closed the door, locked it, and came towards me...

"Mr. Osgood..." I breathed as he pulled me into his arms...

"Yes Mrs. Osgood?" Bazil said as he began kissing me...

"Not... here..." I breathed...

"Then where?" he breathed as he started kissing me on my neck...

"Oooohhh..." I moaned...

"Change your mind?" he asked as he continued kissing my neck...

"I need to get some work done..." I breathed...

"So do I..." he breathed as he began unbuttoning my blouse...

"Let's go home Bazil..." I breathed...

"Are you sure?" Bazil breathed as he continued kissing my neck and began massaging my breast...

"Yeesss..." I breathed...

"Yessss... as in don't stop?" Bazil breathed as he kissed me passionately...

"Bazil... I need to get some work done..." I breathed as I tried to pull away from him...

"Come back here..." Bazil breathed as he pulled me back into his arms and held me..."

"I love you Bazil..."

"I love you too Beautiee..."

"As soon as I'm finished... we can go home..."

"You promise?" he breathed in my ear...

"Yesss... Bazil..." I moaned...

"Okay... I'm going home now... I'll be waiting for you to join me... don't keep me waiting too long... okay?" he breathed as he pulled me into a deep passionate kiss...

"Okay Bazil..." I breathed, silently thanking God he let me go when he did... "Whew! Now I can concentrate..." I said out loud as I went back to work...

"Hey Bazil," Troy said as Bazil got out the car and headed up the driveway...

"Hey Troy..."

"Where's Beautiee?"

"She's still at work..."

"Oh okay – I gotta get back to work – I'll see you later..."

"Aiight Troy..." Bazil said as he went inside... "Let me get upstairs and get ready for Beautiee..." Bazil said out loud as he went upstairs and into the bedroom. As soon as Bazil got upstairs, he stripped out of his clothes and went to take a nice hot shower. When he was done he came out the bathroom...

"Hello Bazil..." MaryJane said as she came out the closet completely naked...

"What the fuck are you doing here MaryJane?" Bazil asked as he went to grab her by the arm...

23

"Uh Uh Uh..." she said playfully as she pulled back the sheets and blankets and climbed in the bed...

"Get the fuck outta here MaryJane..." Bazil growled as lunged towards the bed...

"That's more like it!" MaryJane yelled as she surprised Bazil by pulling him down on top of her...

"Bitch are you crazy?" he yelled as he jumped up off of her... "Beautiee... wait!" I looked at her lying in the bed under the sheet pulled up to her chin, terrified... "I can explain..." he said as he started walking towards me. I watched him walk towards me... slowly and cautiously, in all his glorious splendor, sweat gleaming from every chiseled inch of his body...

"I know everything I need to know..." I said as I raised my arm and aimed the gun at her head...

"Please don't kill me..." she pleaded as if she was relevant...

"Beautiee... please put the gun down..." Bazil pleaded as he inched closer to me and touched my right arm... and I fired... Bang! I watched the blood ooze from her head, relieved that I was smart enough to put the silencer on before I entered the room. I picked up the gun again, pointing it directly at Bazil... "Beautiee... she didn't mean anything..." he pleaded as he backed away from me...

"I know..." I said mischievously as I sat down on the edge of the bed between her legs...

"Come here..." I commanded. Bazil did as I commanded and I was more turned on by the fear in his eyes than I was by his body...

"Beautiee..." he started to say something but I interrupted him by grabbing him by his ass and pulling him towards my mouth. I took his dick in my mouth slowly, circling it with my tongue while simultaneously sliding the gun on the back of his ass with my left hand, and massaging the other side of his ass with my right...

"Fuck my mouth Bazil..." I pleaded while looking into his eyes... Bazil grabbed my head with both his hands and did as he was told, but he wasn't fully erect. I knew he was afraid, I knew he was freaking out because he had his dick in my mouth while the body of his dead lover was right behind me, but I didn't give a damn – this was my dick and I was going to have it... "I love it when you get hard in my mouth Bazil..." I said as I slurped and sucked slowly and deliberately... "That's it Bazil..." I said as he grabbed my head, closed his eyes, rolled his head back, and began fucking my mouth ferociously... and then I stopped suddenly...

"Damn Beautiee... you gonna do me like this... and just stop before I bust a nut?" he breathed. I didn't answer him. I lay back on the bed between his dead lover's legs, using her pelvis as a prop for my head... "What the fuck..." he started to say before I interrupted him...

"Take off my clothes Bazil..." I commanded...

"Whhhaaattt?"

"I said take off my clothes Bazil..." I knew he was freaking out... and it turned me on. He put his hands on my waist and slid my pants and panties to the floor....

"Your pussy is wet... and I'm thirsty..." he growled as he began to devour me... "Who's pussy is this?" he growled...

"Mine..." I moaned...

"You sure about that?" he said as he went back to sucking, licking, and slurping...

"Yeeesss....." I moaned as I rode his face. As I continued to enjoy wave after wave of orgasmic pleasure, he began sliding his hands up my body, thinking he was slick as he inched towards my left hand with the gun in it... "Fuck me Bazil..." I breathed as I tightened my grip on the gun. He slid his hands back down my body, propped himself up, and slammed his dick inside me...

"Is this what you want?" he growled...

"Yes Bazil... Yeeesss!" I screamed as I pulled him down on top of me, on top of his dead lover, tightly gripping the gun, making sure he could feel the cold steel in his back from my left hand and my nails digging into his ass from my right... "Is this my pussy now?" he growled as he continued slamming his dick inside me, sending me past the point of no return, past the orgasmic plateau, and into the orgasmic tornado...

"Yes! Yes! Yeeesssss! I screamed out as my orgasm was so intense it hurt...

"Damn right it is!" he said as he snatched the gun out my hand and continued thrusting... "What's up now Beautiee?" he asked mischievously as he lay on top of me, thrusting slower, but not stopping...

"Cum for me Bazil..." I moaned as I continued to enjoy mini orgasms...

"I'll cum when I'm ready..." he growled as he picked up the pace and picked up his hand to show me he had the gun...

"Yes Bazil... Yeeesss...." I moaned as he thrust harder and faster... he dropped back down on top of me, sliding his right hand up under my blouse, freeing my breasts, licking and sucking them as we both came together...

"Uggh! Uggh! Ugggggghhhh!" Bazil collapsed on top of me, kissing me for a few moments before he spoke... "What's up now Bautiee?" he asked as we continued to lay on top of his dead lover's body...

"Well..." I said matter-of-factly... "You can clean up this mess after I clean myself up and get outta here...

"The fuck you mean?!" Bazil asked as he jumped up off of me, shocked by what I said...

"You need to get rid of that gun – since your finger prints are on it – you need to get rid of that Bitch – and – while you're at it – you need to get rid of that mattress..." I said as I got up and went to the bathroom to clean myself up.

Bazil didn't say a word as I cleaned myself up, got dressed, and headed downstairs towards the door... "Bazil?" I called out before I opened the door to leave...

"Yes Beautiee?"

"Try not to fuck anybody else while I'm out..." I said as I slammed the door...

# Chapter 3

"Yes Bazil?" Trevor said as he answered the phone...

"I need you..."

"I'll be right there..." Trevor said as he hung up, hurried out his apartment to his car, and sped off to get to Bazil...

"Thank God you're here..." Bazil said as he opened the door...

"Baby... you're shaking... come here..." Trevor said as he pulled Bazil into a hug and held him. Bazil held on to Trevor, still shaking, and put his head on Trevor's shoulder... "Bazil... tell me... what's wrong?"

"She scared the fuck outta me..."

"Who?"

"Beautiee..."

"What happened Bazil?"

"I need a drink..."

"Okay..." Trevor said as he followed Bazil into the library and watched Bazil pour two shots...

"Here..." Bazil said as he handed Trevor a shot of Jack Daniels. Trevor didn't speak until they both finished their shots and sat down...

"Baby... please tell me what's going on..."

"It started at the office..."

"Okay..."

"Beautiee heard MaryJane tell another employee she was going to check her as soon as Beautiee got comfortable..."

"Oh shit!"

"That's not all..."

"Okay..."

"MaryJane also told the employee that Beautiee may be my wife for now... but it's only temporary..."

"Oh my God... Bazil..."

"I didn't know anything about this... Beautiee was on her way to the office to tell me..."

"Okay..."

"When she got there... MaryJane was in my office..."

"Oh my God..."

"I had to choke MaryJane to remind her who the fuck she was talking to..."

"Bazil... No...."

"I didn't hurt her..."

"Oh – thank God..."

"But I asked her if I made myself clear... and she said she was as clear as she was when she had my dick in her mouth..."

"Damn Bazil..."

"And Beautiee heard her..."

"Oh my God! What happened?"

"Beautiee came charging into the office... snatched her by her hair... dragged her to the door... and told her she had 10 seconds to get the fuck up and get the hell off the premises..."

"I fuckin' love Beautiee!"

"I love her too... but I'm not finished..."

"Oh no..."

"Beautiee told her if she ever caught her near me again she'd blow her fuckin' head off..."

"Oh shit!"

"She warned me that she'd make good on her promise..."

"Is that what scared you?"

"No... to be honest... I didn't think I'd ever see her again..."

"Bazil!"

"I didn't do anything... I didn't want to..."

"So what happened?"

"She filed for unemployment..."

"Fuckin' Bitch!"

"Exactly..."

"Does Beautiee know?"

"She filled out the denial..."

"Damn Bazil – where'd you find her?"

"She was given to me by God..."

"I've never seen you like this..."

"Like what?"

"You really love her..."

"I do..."

"So what happened?"

"I thought we were done but Sam suggested I call Smalls... so I did..."

"Sounds like good advice..."

"He told me to record my conversations so I had Sam get me a Bluetooth cellphone recorder..."

"Good..."

"She called me..."

"Oh Hell No!"

"She tried to threaten me with rape allegations..."

"Fuckin' Bitch!"

"I kept telling her I wasn't interested in playing with anyone but my wife..."

"Damn Baby... you finally found the one..."

"She thought it was a game..."

"What happened Baby?" Trevor asked as he took Bazil's hand...

"I left work early to come home... Beautiee was on her way..."

"Well that sounds nice..."

"I came out the shower... and she was here..."

"Who was here?"

"MaryJane..."

"Bazil!"

"I DIDN'T INVITE HER IN!" Bazil growled...

"I'm sorry Baby... calm down..." Trevor said as he rubbed Bazil's arm..."

"I told her to leave... I tried to grab her... she pulled away from me... and got in the bed..."

"Oh Hell No!"

"I went to grab her... she pulled me down on top of her... and..."

"Baby... what happened?"

"Beautiee..." Bazil whispered as he started to cry...

"Oh Baby... I'm sorry..." Trevor said as he tried to comfort Bazil...

"Trevor... stop..."

"Okay..."

"Beautiee saw us in bed..."

"Oh shit!"

"I tried to get her to put the gun down..."

"Wait... what did you say?"

"I tried to get her to put the gun down..."

"Bazil... is MaryJane dead?"

"Yes..."

"Oh my poor Baby..."

"She wouldn't put the gun down..."

"Bazil... nooo..."

"She sat down on the bed..."

"Oh my God!"

"She wouldn't let go of the gun until I fucked her..."

"Wait... WHAT?!"

"I know... it's crazy... I was terrified... but I was also turned on..."

"Bazil?"

"Yes Trevor?"

"Where's the gun?"

"It's upstairs... with MaryJane..."

"What did you say?"

"The gun... is upstairs... with MaryJane..."

"In your bed?"

"Yes..."

"How... what..."

"I fucked her... until I could take the gun away from her..."

"Do you think she was going to kill you?"

"No..."

"So why wouldn't she let go of the gun?"

"Because she wanted to let me know she could've killed me..."

"And that's what scares you..." Trevor said as he pulled Bazil into a hug and held him...

"Yesss..."

"Let's go upstairs..."

"Okay..." Bazil said as he followed Trevor upstairs...

"Oh my God..." Trevor whispered...

"Did you bring everything with you?"

"Yes..."

"Where is it?"

"It's in the car..."

"I'll wait here..." Bazil said as Trevor went out to the car. When Trevor came back upstairs he had an extra-large black suitcase with a pull handle and wheels. Bazil watched as Trevor climbed up on the bed, took a cigarette lighter out of his pocket, stripped down to his bare ass, and dropped his clothes in the suitcase. Bazil continued to watch as Trevor went to work on MaryJane's dead body. He started by grabbing her head and breaking her neck. From there he broke both her arms at the elbows and then he broke both her wrists. He moved down further and took the left leg, broke the knee, and then did the same thing with the right. When he got to the feet, he snapped both the ankles. Bazil continued to watch as Trevor bent MaryJane's body in half, push her off the bed into the suitcase, and then contorted her body to make her fit. Trevor stood up and stripped the bed of the sheets, pillows, and blankets, and then dropped them in the suitcase along with the gun on top of MaryJane's dead body. After Trevor closed the suitcase and locked it, he took the lighter and used it to burn the mattress where MaryJane's blood had stained it.

"What's that for?" Bazil asked...

"If anyone askes – you fell asleep with a lit cigarette," Trevor answered. When Trevor was done burning the mattress he walked towards Bazil... "I need a fresh change of clothes..." Trevor said as he headed towards the shower...

"Guess I'll order another mattress," Bazil said out loud as he picked up the phone..."

"Thank you for calling Raymour and Flanigan, this is Nancy..."

"Hello Nancy... this is Mr. Osgood..."

"Mr. Osgood! How Are You!"

"I'm married..."

"Congratulations!"

"Thank you..."

"What can we do for you today?"

"I need a new mattress..."

"Hmmmmm... you just purchased one recently... is there something wrong?"

"My wife is uncomfortable..."

"Oh dear – I'm sorry to hear that – we can exchange it for another if you like..."

"Thanks for the offer but it's been damaged..."

"Well that's too bad – tell you what – let me find you something of equal quality and value and I'll see if I can apply my discount..."

"That would be nice..."

"It's the least we can do for one of our best customers..."

"I appreciate that..."

"Ohhh... this is nice... Stearns & Foster Estate La Fiorentini IV Luxury Cushion Firm Pillowtop Mattress... oh shoot – I can't apply my discount because it's already on sale..."

"That's fine... I believe my wife would like that..."

"Okay – you have two options – you can have the King for $1999 or the California King for $2199..."

"I'll take the California King..."

"Okay – would you like the Low Profile Base or the High Profile Base?"

"I'll take the High Profile Base..."

"Great! Your total is $2439 – do you need that delivered?"

"Yes Nancy..."

"Okay – how soon do you need this delivered?"

"I need it today..."

"I'm sorry Mr. Osgood – I don't have anyone available to deliver it to you today – can you do it tomorrow?"

"I need my wife to sleep comfortably as soon as possible..."

"I'm so sorry Mr. Osgood..."

"No apologies necessary – do you have it available in the store?"

"As a matter of fact, we do!"

"How soon can I pick it up?"

"You can pick it up within the hour..."

"Okay Nancy... thank you..."

"You're welcome Mr. Osgood – thank you for shopping with us..."

"Are you okay?" Trevor asked as he came out the shower..."

"Yea..."

"Who was on the phone?"

"Hold on a minute – that's Raymour and Flanigan," Bazil said as the phone rang... "Nancy?"

"Oh thank God – I can get your mattress delivered to you later today – we had a cancellation – but it'll be about 2 hours – is that okay?"

"That's fine – thank you Nancy..."

"You're welcome Mr. Osgood..." she said as Bazil hung up the phone...

"Good – now that you have that out of the way – commere..." Trevor said as he pulled Bazil into a kiss..."

"Mmmmmm.... Bazil moaned as he moved his hands down Trevor's body...

"Baby... I wish we could... but I need to take care of MaryJane..." Trevor said between kisses...

"We have time..." Bazil breathed as he pushed Trevor down on the bed, climbed on top of him, and continued kissing him...

"Bazil... Baby... we can't..." Trevor said as he pushed Bazil off of him, stood up, and started getting dressed...

"I know..." Bazil sighed...

"I'll see you soon..." Trevor said as he pulled Bazil into another kiss..."

"Thank you Trevor..." Bazil breathed...

"You're welcome Baby... I love you...

"I love you too..." Bazil said as Trevor took the suitcase, bounced it down the stairs, and left the house. Bazil sat there for about another hour or so, deep in thought, until he heard a knock at the door... "Who is it?"

"Raymour and Flannigan..."

"Come on in guys..." Bazil said as he opened the door...

"Where to Sir?"

"Follow me..." Bazil said as they followed him upstairs into the bedroom...

"Is this the mattress we're removing?"

"Yes..."

"Okay – we'll get this outta your way and then we'll set up the new one for you..."

"Sounds good..." Bazil said as they went to work. Once they got the old mattress out they brought the new one in, set it up, cleaned up their mess, and went to leave... "Here you go..." Bazil said as he handed them $100 each...

"Thank you Sir!" they said – first one and then the other....

"Have a nice day," Bazil said as he closed the door and went back upstairs...

"Now to make this up before Beautiee gets home..." he said out loud as he started making up the bed. When he was done the phone rang...

"Bazil..."

"Beautiee... what's wrong?" Bazil asked with concern in his voice...

"Bazil..."

"Beautiee... where are you?"

"I'm sitting... right... here..." I slurred...

"Beautiee... where are you sitting?"

"Bazil... I'm sitting... at the bar... tee hee hee..."

"Beautiee – where's the car?"

"I... don't... remember..."

"Beautiee – did you drive the car?"

"Yeeesss....."

"Did you park the car?"

"Duuuhhh... tee hee hee..."

"Beautiee – let me speak to the bartender..."

"Excussseeee meeee...." I slurred as I tried to get the bartender's attention... "He... won't... answer... me..."

"Beautiee – stay there – I'm on my way..."

"Okay Bazil..." I slurred as I hung up...

"Yes Bazil?" Trevor answered...

"How was lunch?"

"Lunch was good..."

"Glad to hear it – I need you to come back to the house right away..."

"What's wrong Baby?"

"Beautiee called – she needs me to come get her..."

"Where is she?"

"She's at Fridays..."

"Is she okay?"

"She can't drive..."

"Okay – I'm on my way..."

"Excussseeee meeee...." I slurred again...

"Yes Miss?" the bartender answered with a smile...

"Do... you... have... my... keys..."

"I'm sorry Maam... I can't let you drive..."

"I... need... you... to... give... my... keys... to... my... husband..."

"Is he here?"

"He's... on... his... way..."

"Okay Maam..."

"I need... another... drink..."

"I think you've had enough Maam..."

"May... I... have... another... drink... please?"

"I'll be right with you Maam..." the bartender said as he walked over to speak with the manager... "She's asking for another drink..."

"Is she over 21?"

"Yes... but she's pretty drunk already..."

"Do you have her keys?"

"Yes..."

"Is she being belligerent?"

"No... but I think she's had enough..."

"I'm sure she has – but she's not being belligerent and she's not driving so go ahead and give it to her..."

"Okay..." the bartender said as he came back over to me...

"Here... my husband... wants... to talk... to... you..." I slurred as I handed him the phone...

"There's nobody on the phone Maam..." he said as he handed the phone back to me and Bazil walked in...

"Heeeyyy my Thirst Quencher..." I slurred as I stumbled into his arms...

"Hey Beautiee..." Bazil laughed as he held me up...

"Have a drink with me..." I slurred...

"Okay Beautiee... let's sit you down..." Bazil laughed as he sat me on the stool...

"What can I get you?" the bartender asked...

"I'll have whatever she's drinking..." Bazil answered.

"Long Island Ice Tea – coming right up..." he said as he prepared the drink for Bazil.

"How many drinks has she had?" Bazil asked...

"That's her third one..." the bartender laughed...

"Does she have a tab?" Bazil asked...

"No – she has a Black American Express..."

"I'll take that card..."

"Sir – I can't give it to you unless I see ID..." the bartender said as he placed Bazil's drink on the counter...

"You didn't ask me for ID to make me this drink – but you need to see ID to give me my card? That's funny..." Bazil laughed as he began drinking...

"Excussseeee meeee.... Bartender..." I slurred..."

"Yes Maam?"

"You can give him the card... he's... my... husband..."

"Okay Maam – sorry about that – here's your card sir..."

"C'mon Beautiee... let's get you home..."

"Okay... my... Thirst Quencher..." I sighed. When we got outside we got into an Uber... "Where's the car?" I slurred...

"I have someone coming to pick it up..." Bazil answered as he helped me into the back seat, sat beside me, and held me...

"I'm sorry Bazil..." I said as I started to cry...

"Ssshhh... it's okay Beautiee..." he said as he kissed my face...

"Do you still love me?"

"I'll always love you..." he said as he continued to kiss my face...

"I love you... my Thirst Quencher..."

"I love you too..." he said as he began kissing me in my mouth to keep me from talking. When we got home he picked me up and carried me to the front door...

"Is she alright?" Trevor asked...

"Yea – she's okay..." Bazil answered as Trevor unlocked the door for Bazil... "Thank you Trevor – I don't know what I'd do without you..." Bazil said as he carried me into the house, upstairs, and into the bedroom... "Let's get you to bed Beautiee..." Bazil said as he undressed me..."

"Yesss... my Thirst Quencher..." I sighed... "This bed is soooo comfortable... are you coming?"

"Is that what you want?" Bazil asked as he pulled the covers up around me...

"Yeessss.... My Thirst Quencher..." I sighed...

"Okay..." Bazil said as he got undressed, climbed in bed, and held me as I drifted off to sleep.

# Chapter 4

"Good evening..." Bazil breathed in my ear as he kissed me awake. "How are you feeling?" he asked as he ran his left hand over my breasts and down to my stomach...

"I'm feeling good..." I breathed as I pulled him closer to my body...

"Mmmmmm... you do feel good..." Bazil breathed as he climbed on top of me...

"Bazil..." I moaned as he slid himself inside me...

"Yeeesss.... Beautiee..." he moaned as he began thrusting. I spread my legs wider and ran my hands down to the small of his back, holding on tight... I tried to moan out loud but Bazil deliberately covered my mouth with his, tonging me down fiercely... "Mmmmmph! Mmmmmph! Mmmmmph!"

"MmmmMmmm...      MmmmMmmm... MmmmMmmm..."

"Mmmmmph! Mmmmmph! Mmmmmph!"

"MmmmMmmm...      MmmmMmmm... MmmmMmmm..." I brought my legs up, locked my feet together around Bazil's back, and held him down on top of me as he continued thrusting, slower and deeper...

"Mmmmmph! Mmmmmph! Mmmmmph!"

"MmmmMmmm... MmmmMmmm... MmmmMmmm..." Bazil slid his arms underneath me, holding on to me by my shoulders, continuing to tongue me down while keeping pace with me, still thrusting slower and deeper...

"Mmmmmph! Mmmmmph! Mmmmmph!"

"MmmmMmmm... MmmmMmmm... MmmmMmmm..." Bazil knew I was coming so he started to pick up the pace and the intensity of his thrusting and stroking... "Mmmmmph! Mmmmmph! Mmmmmph!" I unclasped my feet from around Bazil's back and lowered my legs but I continued to hold him down on top of me as we continued kissing, tonging each other down as our orgasms subsided... until Bazil spoke...

"Are you hungry?" he asked as we continued kissing..."

"Yeesss..." I breathed...

"I made dinner..."

"It smells delicious..."

"Let's go downstairs..."

"Do we have to?"

"Nooo... we... can... stay here... if that's... what... you... want..."

"I need... to... eat..."

"Are... you... sure?" Bazil asked as I could feel him getting hard again inside me...

"Bazil..." I moaned...

"Yeeesss.... Beautiee..." Bazil answered as he began thrusting slowly..."

"Oh Bazil..." I moaned as he continued kissing me...

"Yes... Beautiee..." Bazil breathed as he began thrusting harder and deeper..."

"I'm cumming Bazil..."

"I'm cumming with you..."

"Ooooohhhhh..."

"Uuugh!"

"Oooohhhh...."

Uuugh!"

Oooooohhhhh....."

"Uuugh!"

"Oooohhh....."

"Uuugh!" Bazil collapsed on top of me as we continued kissing... until I spoke...

"Bazil..."

"Yesss... Beautiee..."

"I... need... to... tell... you... something..."

"Okay..." Bazil said as he stopped kissing me and looked at me...

"I feel like I felt when you asked me to marry you..."

"Oh Beautiee..." Bazil whispered as his eyes filled with tears...

"I love you sooo much Bazil..." I said as my eyes filled with tears...

"I love you too..." Bazil said as he pulled me to him and kissed me hard...

"Bazil..."

"Yes Beautiee..."

"Let's eat..."

"Are you sure?"

"Yes... I'm hungry..."

"So am I..." Bazil said as he took my right breast in his mouth while massaging my left breast...

"Bazil..." I moaned... "I need to eat..."

"Okay..." he said as he continued to suck on and fondle my breasts... "But after I feed you... I need more... dessert..."

"Mmmmmm.... Okay...." I moaned as I arched my back...

"C'mon..." Bazil said as he got up and pulled me up with him. Bazil gave me one of his robes, he put on the other robe, and we went downstairs to the kitchen...

"Oh Bazil!" I gasped when I saw the table. Two candles had burned down a bit but there was still plenty left as I sat at the table. Bazil poured us both a glass of chardonnay and set those on the table before serving us Cesar salad. "Mmmmmm...." I said as we ate...

"I'm glad you're enjoying it..." Bazil said as he smiled. When we were done with the Cesar salad, Bazil served us steak, potatoes au gratin, and garlic bread.

"Oh my God... this is so good..." I moaned as I ate. Bazil didn't say anything – he just smiled as we finished our food. "Bazil?"

"Yes Beautiee?"

"I need to ask you something..."

"Okay..."

48

"How did MaryJane get in here?" I watched as Bazil's demeanor changed completely...

"She had a key..." he sighed with his head down...

"Did you invite her here?"

"No..."

"Bazil?"

"Yes Beautiee?"

"Does anyone else have a key?"

"Yes..."

"Who?"

"Trevor..."

"Your best friend..."

"Beautiee?"

"Yes Bazil?"

"Where'd you get the gun?"

"I've always had it..."

"Where'd you get it?"

"Billie..."

"So it's not registered..."

"No..."

"How long have you..."

"Carried?"

"Yes..."

"Always..."

"I'm sorry..."

"I know..."

"Do you forgive me?"

"Oh Bazil..." I whispered as I got up from my chair and went over to him, pulled him up out the chair, held him, and looked up at him as he held me back... "Yes my Thirst Quencher..."

"I love you so much Beautiee..." Bazil said as he pulled me into a kiss...

"Do you forgive me?" I asked with tears in my eyes...

"Beautiee..." Bazil breathed as he kissed my tears... "There's nothing to forgive...

"Are you ready for more dessert?"

"Always..." Bazil said as he picked me up and carried me upstairs into the bedroom.

# Chapter 5

"Where's Beautiee?" Trevor asked as he came in and closed the door behind him...

"She's at the salon – she'll be gone for a few hours..." Bazil answered as he smiled mischievously...

"Ohhh... that's good... that means I can have dessert..."

"Cumere..." Bazil breathed as he pulled Trevor into a kiss...

"I've missed you..." Trevor breathed in between kisses...

"I've missed you too..." Bazil breathed as he pulled Trevor closer and wrapped his arms around him while continuing to kiss him...

"Mmmmmm..." Trevor moaned as he started rubbing Bazil's dick through his pants. Bazil continued kissing Trevor while pushing him backwards into the library. Bazil pushed Trevor down on the couch, pushed Trevor down on his back, unbuckled his pants, and slid them down to his ankles along with his boxers. Trevor kicked off his shoes, his pants, and his boxers, and then spread his legs. Bazil kneeled on the couch between Trevor's legs, unbuttoned his shirt,

51

unbuckled his belt, dropped his pants and boxers, and showed Trevor his swollen dick. Trevor leaned forward and took it in his mouth...

"Yes... suck it..." Bazil moaned as Trevor sucked his dick feverishly...

"Mmmmmm.... Lay back and spread your legs..." Trevor did as he was told and watched as Bazil tore the condom wrapper, took the condom out, and put it on his dick... "Are you ready for me?" Bazil asked as he stroked his dick...

"Yes Daddy – I'm ready..." Trevor breathed. Bazil lay down on top of Trevor, spread Trevor's ass cheeks, and eased his dick in Trevor's ass slowly...

"I can't believe I went all the way over there just to find out they canceled my appointment..." I sighed as I pulled into the driveway. "Hmmmmm... I see Trevor's car – he must have stopped by to see Bazil..." I said as I got out. I walked up to the door, knocked, and waited... "Hmmmmm... they must be in the library..." I said as I started digging in my pocket book for my keys...

"Oh yes... that's it... Daddy your dick feels so good..." Trevor moaned as Bazil began fucking him...

"Mmmmmm... I've been looking forward to this all day..." Bazil breathed in Trevor's ear as he pulled Trevor closer to him, held on to him by his shoulders, and kissed him passionately...

"Got em!" I said out loud as I opened the door and let myself in... "Bazil – can you believe I went all the way over there just to find out they cancelled my appointment? Bazil? Baby where are you? Oh – I know – in the library getting your drink on huh..." I said as I went towards the library...

"You gonna make me cum Daddy!" I heard Trevor say...

"Cum for Daddy..." I heard Bazil say...

"BAZZZZIIILLL!!! OH MY GODDDD!!!! WHAT THE FUCK ARE YOU DOING????!!!!"

"Beautiee... I can explain..." Bazil said as he jumped up off of Trevor. I grabbed the bottle of scotch and threw it across the library towards the couch where Trevor was scrambling to pull up his pants. The glass broke and broken glass mixed with scotch hit the back of the couch and dripped onto the bottom of the couch and onto the floor. I looked back toward Bazil and I saw him standing there with a condom on his dick.... And I went ballistic... Bazil's eyes got really big as I grabbed a bottle of Hennessey and threw it towards Trevor – and this time I didn't miss...

"Aaaahhh!" Trevor cried out as the bottle hit him in his head. I started laughing maniacally when I saw the gash over Trevor's eye with blood gushing out.  Bazil charged towards me as I grabbed the letter opener...

"I'LL KILL YOU!!!" I screamed as I lunged at Bazil with the letter opener but Bazil jumped out of the way so I ended up stabbing the door instead...

"Beautiee... Baby... please... put that down... you're going to hurt yourself..." Bazil said as Trevor jumped up from the couch and ran out while Bazil had my attention diverted...

"You're right..." I said calmly... "I should put this down... and you should clean this mess up... I'm going out... I'll be back later..." I said as I picked up my keys, put my pocket book on my shoulder, and went to sit in the car... "Mutha Fuckin' best friend my ass – NO! – His ass!" I said as I started laughing maniacally... "Le'me git ole girl and put her in my purse..." I said as I opened the glove compartment... "Ahhh... there's my baby girl..." I said as I took the gun out of the glove compartment and held it up to my eyes... "We have business to attend to..." I said as I kissed the gun, put it in my purse, put the car in drive, and drove straight to the Holiday Inn Express.

"I need a room please!" I snapped when I got to the counter...

"Do you have a reservation maam?"

"No..." I sighed...

"Let me see if we have anything available... hmmmmm... I'm sorry... we're booked solid..."

"Please... I really need a room... I'll take anything..." I pleaded as my eyes filled with tears..."

"Well... we have a King Leisure Suite available... if they don't check in..."

"What time is check-in?"

"Check-in starts at 4pm and ends at 9pm... unless you call to ask us to extend it... then it can go up to midnight..."

"Did you get a call to request a late check-in?"

"Nope... and it will be 9pm in 5... 4... 3...2...1 – now we just wait for the room to be released and... okay – I can check you in right now!" She smiled...

"Thank you soooo much... I really appreciate it..." I breathed as I gave her my Black Card...

"Mrs. Osgood! Oh my goodness – why didn't you say so! It's so nice to finally meet you in person! I'm Shireen!" she said as she came from behind the counter to give me a hug...

"Nice to meet you Shireen..." I said as I hugged her back... "So you know my husband?"

"Yes I do... he comes here with Trevor whenever they have business..."

"Is that right?" I asked as my blood began to boil...

"Yea — they come here for drinks too — Trevor is fine — if I wasn't already married he could definitely git it — oh my God — I can't believe I just said that — excuse me!"

"Oh that's okay Shireen — we can keep it between us girls..." I laughed as I took my card and my key...

"Have a good night — nice meeting you!" she yelled as I went towards the elevator...

"Mutha fucka been fuckin' Trevor here huh — thanks for telling me Shireen!" I gritted as I punched the button for my floor. When the doors opened, I got off the elevator and saw my room was to the right... "Good — easy to find..." I said as I opened the door and went into the room... "I need a drink..." I said as I went straight to the bar. My cell phone started ringing so I picked it up and saw it was Bazil... "Fuck You Mutha Fucka!" I yelled as I threw the phone on the bed and poured myself a glass of Jack Daniels... "Aaahhh yess... just what I needed..." I said as I gulped it down. I sat on the bed, picked up my cell phone, and called Trevor...

"Baby... is that you?" he answered...

"It's me Baby..." I answered eerily...

"Beautiee... how'd you get this number?"

"Meet me at the Holiday Inn Express..."

"Hell no Bitch — you just tried to take my fuckin' head off — are you crazy?"

"You fucked my husband — I tried to take your fuckin' head off — one good fuck deserves another... and I'm on a mission to collect..."

"Wait... What?"

"I want you to fuck me Trevor..."

"Are you serious?"

"I'm in room 432..." I answered... and then hung up. I poured myself another drink, gulped it down, lay down on the bed, and fell asleep.

# Chapter 6

"Mmmmy.... Bazil... somebody's at the door..." I yawned as I stretched... "Shit – I forgot where the hell I was for a sec..." I said as I got up to answer the door. "Come in Trevor..." I said as I opened the door. Trevor came into the room, closed the door behind him, and walked towards the bar...

"Mind if I pour myself a drink?"

"Help yourself – and pour me another one while you're at it..." I said as I walked over to the bar, took the glass from him, and gulped it down...

"Thirsty huh?" Trever asked as he sipped his drink...

"Finish your drink Trevor..." I demanded as I pulled back the blankets and sheets, sat on the bed, and started undressing myself. Trevor did as he was told, stood up, and started to undress. I climbed into the bed, propped myself up, and watched Trevor get completely nude...

"Do you like what you see?" Trevor asked as he stood in front of me.

"As a matter-of-fact... I do – come here..." Trevor came towards the bed and I sat up and grabbed his dick...

"Mmmmmm... that feels nice..." Trevor said as I played with his dick...

"It certainly does – get in here..." I said as I moved over to the middle of the bed...

"Yes maam..." he said as he got in bed, pulled up the covers, and pulled me close to him... "You're so beautiful..." he whispered as he pulled me into a kiss..."

"Le'me ask you something..." I said before he kissed me again...

"Yes Beautiee..." Trevor breathed as he began kissing me on my neck...

"Am I your first?"

"Yes Beautiee..."

"Le'me ask you something else..." I said before he kissed me again...

"Yes Beautiee..." Trevor breathed as he moved down to my left breast...

"Did you suck Bazil's dick?"

"Yes..." he answered while sucking on my breast...

"So did I..." I laughed... "Le'me ask you another question..." I said as Trevor moved to my right breast and started fondling and sucking it...

"Yes Beautiee..." he answered as he alternated between licking and fondling my breasts...

"Did Bazil suck your dick?"

"Yes..."

"Le'me ask you another question..."

"Okay..." Trevor sighed as he propped himself up beside me...

"Did you ever stop and think that every time you kissed Bazil..." I asked as I pulled him into a kiss... "You're tasting my pussy?"

"Ummmmm... no... I umm... I never thought about that..." he answered nervously...

"Well..." I said as I pulled him back into a kiss... "Now that I know Bazil sucked your dick..." I said before I kissed him again... "I know I've been tasting you too..."

"How does that make you feel?" Trevor asked as he climbed on top of me and spread my legs...

"Fuck me and I'll tell you..." I breathed...

"As you wish..." he said as he got up on his knees, opened the condom wrapper, put the condom on, laid back down on top of me, spread my legs a bit further, and eased his dick inside me... "Mmmmmm..." he moaned in my ear as he started fucking me slowly. I thought he was going to fuck me as though he didn't give a damn – especially because I bust him in his head and split it open – but he wasn't actually fucking me at all – he was making love to me – well – his version of it anyway... "You feel so good..." he breathed in my ear...

"Do I?"

"Yeesss..." he moaned and then went back to stroking...

"Okay Trevor..." I thought to myself as he picked up the pace a bit... "Might as well enjoy this..." I thought as I closed my eyes, moved my hands down his back, and threw the pussy back at him. Trevor took that as a sign that we was putting it on me and picked up the pace a bit more. He had a nice dick - and I was enjoying it – but he's no Bazil...

"You like that?" he breathed...

"Yes... I like that..." He continued stroking me while kissing me on my neck and licking on my earlobes and I started to giggle...

"Does that tickle?" he breathed...

"Yes... it does..." I moaned a little...

"Oh Beautiee..." he moaned before he kissed me fully in the mouth. He had nice, soft lips and he was definitely a good kisser and as I kissed him back, my body betrayed me. I tried to keep my orgasm to myself but my pussy did what pussy do – it tightened and contracted around his dick... "That's it Beautiee... cum for me..." he breathed in my ear before kissing me again... and I was defeated...

"Yes... that's it... right there... don't stop... don't stop... I'm cummmmiiinnggg.... Ooohhhh.... Oooohhhhhh Yeeessss!" Trevor continued stroking me as he turned my face to his so he could look me in my eyes. I could tell he was pleased with himself but he wasn't looking at me with malice – he was looking at me with love. Trevor pulled my face to his, kissed me again, and then buried his face in my neck as he stroked me harder...

"Oh shit – your pussy feels so damn good... I'm cummmmmiiinnnggg! Uggghhhh!" He continued to lay on top of me, kissing me softly, and I didn't push him off of me – because I didn't want to... "Can I make you cum again?"

"Sure..." I breathed. I thought he was going to put on a condom and go for round 2 but he had something else in mind... "Wwwhhaattt... are you doing?" I asked as he started kissing his way down my body...

"Just relax... and enjoy..." he said as he spread my lips and dove in...

"Oh Trevor!" I moaned. Trevor continued licking, sucking, and slurping. His mouth and tongue felt good and I didn't want him to stop... "Trevor... I'm cumming again... ooohhh... ooohhh... ooohhh... ooohhh... Aaagggh!" I moaned as I arched my back up off the bed and back down...

"Mmmmmm... that was good..." Trevor said as he licked his lips while coming up from in between my legs to lay beside me...

"It certainly was..." I said as I got up out the bed and went to the bathroom. When I came out the bathroom I threw a red towel at him...

"Come back to bed... we have the rest of the night..." he said as he started wiping his crotch...

"No thank you... thanks though..." I said.
"Oh... it's like that?"

"Like what?"

"So... you're finished?"

"Basically..."

"Oh that's fucked up..."

"Oh please – men do it all the time..."

"Your pussy wasn't that good anyway," he chuckled as I stood there in front of him with my hands on my hips, legs spread apart.

"Still gay huh?" I asked as I snatched the red towel from his crotch and proceeded to wipe his sweat from my pubic hair.

"I wasn't finished," he laughed as he sat up in the bed.

"Here you go," I said as I tossed the towel in his face playfully."

"So why didn't you suck my dick?"

"That's his job," I answered matter-of-factly.

"Oh I see," he laughed. "You just wanted me to fuck you..."

"Exactly..."

"Why?"

"Why not?"

"What's that supposed to mean?"

"You just don't get it..." I sighed with a quizzical look.

"Why'd you do this?"

"I wanted what my husband had."

"Is that the only reason?"

"Why did you?" I asked sarcastically.

"Look – I didn't mean to fall in love with your husband... it just happened..."

"Don't give me that bullshit mutha fucka!" I growled.

"I didn't mean..."

"I don't give a fuck what you meant!" I said as I climbed up on the bed, straddled him again, reached down in my purse to get my gun, cocked it, and pointed it at the head board.

"Oh God, please don't kill me," he moaned...

"Relax Baby..." I cooed in his ear... "I came here to fuck you – not kill you..." I whispered as I ran my tongue from his earlobe down to his neck...

"Oh God... No... you're going to kill him aren't you?" he screamed as he jumped up in the bed, knocking me into the night stand.

"You son-of-a-bitch!" I screamed as I jumped up and swung my hand, slapping the taste out of his mouth.

"What do you want from me?" he moaned as he started crying.

"I thought you said you were the man," I laughed. He jumped up off the bed and he startled me as he grabbed me by the shoulders, slammed my back against the wall, and put his face to mine.

"Don't ever question my manhood again Bitch," he breathed.

"Mutha fucka – who you think you talkin' too?" I laughed as I stared him down. "You been fuckin' my husband for weeks – all the while pretending to be my friend – I call you and tell you I want you to fuck me and you come running – you know what – I'm done with this – get the fuck off me," I laughed as I pushed him away from me and grabbed my clothes.

"I'm not done with you," he said as he snatched me by the wrist.

"You wanna catch a charge mutha fucka?"

"I'm sorry," he said as he let go of my wrist and I started getting dressed.

"I don't believe this shit," I laughed. "If you were any type of man, when I called you and told you I wanted you to fuck me you would've told me hell no," I laughed again.

"I did tell you hell no... at first..."

"So why'd you fuck me then?"

"Because I felt sorry for you..." he laughed.

"You fucked me because you wanted to – because you wanted me..." I said matter-of-factly. "You've been fuckin' my husband for weeks – hell – for all I know – you probably fuckin' other men too – he can't trust you any more than I can trust him..." I laughed.

"It's not what you think!" he yelled.

"What the fuck is it then?" I yelled back. "Have you been fuckin' my husband or not?"

"I love him!" he yelled.

"You what?" I asked as I got up in his face.

"I love him," he sighed as he sat down and covered his face with his hands... "And I love you too..."

"You love me? Since when?"

"I've always loved you Beautiee," he said as he tried to put his hand on my shoulder.

"You've got major issues," I laughed as I pushed his hand off my shoulder.

"I'm serious Beautiee."

"Well – you've got a fucked up way of showing it," I laughed.

"I never meant to hurt you...," he sighed.

"Yea – you and Bazil have that in common," I laughed.

"Look Beautiee... we couldn't help it..."

"Don't waste your breath Trevor," I interrupted as I got up to leave. "Ya know – it's a shame you're not straight," I said as I put my gun in my bag and I put my bag on my shoulder. "You're nice lookin', you have a good job, a nice portfolio, and a nice dick – you could use a refresher course in how to please a woman but overall, I'd say you have potential," I said as I put on my coat and headed towards the door...

"Fuck you Bitch!" he yelled.

"You just did – thanks!" I said as I slammed the door and headed down the corridor towards the elevator.

# Chapter 7

"Well, well, well... look who finally decided to come home," Bazil said as I came in.

"Home? Yea right," I laughed.

"Do you have any idea what time it is?" he asked.

"Is the clock broke?" I answered.

"Don't play with me Beautiee!" he snapped.

"I wasn't planning to," I said.

"Oh you got jokes? Okay..." he said as he got up off the couch and followed me into the kitchen...

"Where's the wine?" I asked as I looked in the cabinets.

"You think you can do whatever-the-fuck you want right?" he asked as he came up behind me and grabbed me by the back of the neck...

"I know I can – now get the fuck off me!" I yelled as I elbowed him in the ribs. When he let go of me to recover from wincing in pain, I slid from between him and the counter and started to run out the kitchen, but he caught me by my hair...

"Get your ass back here Beautiee!" he growled as he yanked me back in the kitchen and threw me into the edge of the granite counter top. When he saw the tears in my eyes he laughed. "I'm gonna make you regret the day you ever met me," he said as he pinned me against the counter with his body, bracing himself against the counter with his right hand.

"I've regretted the day I met you ever since I found out you've been fucking Trevor!" I snapped as I pushed him away from me. He didn't say anything. He just stood there, staring through me as I watched his nostrils flare.

"You had no business fucking him," he breathed as he came towards me again, gritting his teeth.

"You wanna die?" I asked as I grabbed the knife...

"You don't have it in you," he said as he got closer... close enough for me to stab him in his hand...

"Guess again!" I yelled as I plunged the knife into the palm of his left hand on the counter.

"I'll kill you!" he growled as he grabbed the knife out of the palm of his hand and headed towards me with it... but I was backing out of the kitchen towards the living room... and my pocketbook was within my reach... "You're cell phone is over there," he laughed as he pointed across the living room, inching closer to me... but I found what I wanted... cocked it... and pointed it right at him...

"If you fucked him without a condom and caught an STD, I'm already dead!" I yelled...

"Beautiee... please – we both know it's not loaded..." he laughed.

"Guess again!" I yelled as I shot the knife out his hand. The look of fear on him was priceless. "Here's how this is gonna go," I said as I walked up to him... cocked the gun again... put the gun to the right side of his temple... and whispered in his ear... "As long as you live – don't ever touch me again... unless I want you to..."

"Is everything alright?" Keisha asked as she knocked on the door. "Thank you Lord," I said as I opened the door.

"Hey Keisha," I said with my head down.

"Girl, what's wrong?" she asked as she pushed her way into the living room and sat down on the couch. "You're bleeding Bazil – oh my God – what happened?"

"She stabbed me," Bazil answered.

"What?! Is that true Beautiee?"

"Sure is!"

"Call the police Keisha..." Bazil said.

"Somebody already did – it sounded like a gun went off in here."

"Who is it?" I snapped as I heard knocking...

"Police," she said. Bazil stood there giving me the evil eye as I walked towards the door.

"May I help you?" I asked.

"My name is Detective Jones... may I come in?"

"Sure," I said as I opened the door and let her in...

"Hi, I'm Detective Jones... but my friends call me Katina," she said as she extended her hand..."

"I'm Beautiee... and this is my husband Bazil," I said as I pointed over to Bazil...

"We know each other," Bazil said, not moving from where he was standing...

"May I sit?" Katina asked.

"Sure," I said as I sat with her on the couch...

"I'll get you ladies something to drink," Bazil said as he headed towards the kitchen...

"Are you okay?" Katina whispered.

"Yea... I'm just pissed off," I sighed.

"Your neighbor said you were fighting..."

"Yea... we were..."

"I don't see any bruises... did he hurt you?"

"It wasn't that kinda fight," I laughed "We just cursed each other out..."

"Your neighbor said she heard gun shots..."

"I bet she did... we were watching Law and Order," I lied.

"Okay... that makes sense..."

"Ladies," Bazil said as he handed us our drinks... "I gave you ginger ale Katina... I hope that's alright..." Bazil said as I sipped and observed...

"Oh that's fine – I'm on duty," she said as she finished her ginger ale...

"Well... don't let us keep you," Bazil said as he directed her towards the front door...

"Alrighty then," she laughed as she went to leave...

"Bazil?"

"Yes Beautiee?"

"Could you make me another drink while I see Katina out?"

"Sure," Bazil answered as he looked at me perplexed before going back into the kitchen...

"Thanks for stopping by," I said as I opened the door for her to leave...

"Be careful Beautiee," she whispered as she handed me her card... "Your husband's a dangerous man," she whispered again as I closed the door behind her...

"What was that all about?" Bazil asked as he handed me a drink and walked me back towards the living room...

"You..."

"What'd she say?"

"She said I need to be careful because you're dangerous," I answered as I finished my drink...

"I'll be back later Beautiee," Bazil said as he put on his jacket and picked up his keys...

"Bazil?"

"Yes Beautiee?"

"Did you fuck her?"

"Hell no!" he said as he went out, closing the door behind him.

# Chapter 8

"Who is it?" Trevor yelled as he jumped up out of bed...

"Open the fuckin' door," Bazil growled...

"Baby... I can explain..." Bam! Trevor held his face as he struggled to get up off the floor...

"What the fuck did I tell you?" Bazil growled as he grabbed Trevor by the throat and pinned him up against the wall, choking him...

"I can't breathe..." Trevor gasped...

"I guess you don't understand fuckin' English... I warned you..." Bazil growled as he continued squeezing Trevor's throat...

"Please..." As much as Bazil wanted to choke the life out of Trevor... he couldn't... so he stopped choking him and let him drop to the floor. Bazil continued to watch Trevor as he gasped for breath, composing himself. Bazil reached out his hand to help Trevor up off the floor, but Trevor jerked away from him...

"You brought that on yourself," Bazil said.

"No... you brought that on us both," Trevor said as they both walked into the living room and sat down...

"You fucked my wife…"

"She wasn't supposed to be your wife…"

"You still fucked my wife… you crossed the line… I told you I'd kill you…"

"And yet… here I am… alive and breathing…" Trevor said as he tried to kiss Bazil…

"Oh hell no… you can't be fuckin' serious right now!" Bazil yelled as he pushed Trevor away from him…

"I'm sorry Baby… I couldn't help it…"

"What the fuck does that mean?"

"I had no idea it would go that far…"

"Are you saying you didn't fuck her?"

"No…" Trevor said as he hung his head…

"What happened Trevor?" Bazil asked as he leaned in closer to Trevor…

"She called me and said she wanted me to fuck her…"

"Whhhaaattt?!"

"So I agreed to meet her at the Holiday Inn Express. When I got there, I expected her to curse me out, tell me to stay the fuck away from you… like the others…"

"That didn't happen?"

"She had a gun…"

"What?"

"She had a gun Bazil…"

"Wait a minute… she wanted you to meet her at the hotel to kill you?"

"No…"

"Trevor?"

"She said she wanted me to fuck her Bazil..."

"Wait... Wait... Wait... she put a gun to your head and raped you?"

"No... Bazil..."

"Trevor?"

"She said she wanted me to fuck her... "

"So you fucked her?"

"Yes Bazil..." Trevor whispered with tears in his eyes...

"Why Trevor?" Bazil asked with tears in his eyes...

"I never meant to hurt you Baby... I'm sorry," Trevor cried... "But when she said she wanted me... I couldn't help it..." Trevor cried as he put his head in his hands... "She told me she wanted what her husband had..."

"When did you find out she had a gun?"

"I saw it after we were finished..."

"Did you ask her about it?"

"Yes..."

"What'd she say?"

"She said she was there to fuck me... not kill me..."

"Wait... What?"

"She straddled me... told me to relax... and then she told me she was there to fuck me... not kill me...

"Oh my God... I've created a monster," Bazil whispered...

"I knocked her down and asked her if she was going to kill you... and she got really angry because I knocked her on the floor..."

"Did you hurt her?"

"I didn't mean to Baby... I just reacted... I thought she was trying to kill you..."

"That's okay Trevor... but you still shouldn't have fucked her..."

"I know Baby... I'm sorry..."

"Don't EVER let it happen again Trevor..."

"I won't Baby... I promise... I'll make it up to you..." he said as he started kissing Bazil...

"Show me..." Bazil breathed as Trevor began unbuckling Bazil's pants, unzipped his zipper, and pulled out his dick... "Mmmmmm..." Bazil moaned as Trevor stroked Bazil's dick while continuing to kiss him...

"Come here," Bazil commanded as he pulled Trevor down on top of him and they continued kissing... Trevor slid down Bazil's chest to his groin and slowly took Bazil's dick into his mouth... "Yeeessss.... Suck it...." Bazil moaned as he grabbed Trevor's head and guided him up and down...

"Mmmmmm...." Trevor moaned as he quickened the pace...

"Ohhh ssshhhiiittt..... Aaaagggghhhhh...." Bazil growled as Trevor swallowed every drop. "We have a problem..." Bazil said as he pulled Trevor up from between his legs and pulled him back down on top of him...

"What's wrong Baby?" Trevor asked as they held each other...

"Katina..."

"What!?" Trevor yelled as he jumped up off Bazil...

"Come back here..."Bazil commanded as he pulled Trevor back down on top of him and held him...

"What do you need me to do Baby?" Trevor asked as he began kissing Bazil..."

"Nothing... yet..."

"Baby... she's a detective..."

"I know..."

"We     need     to     be     careful..."

"I know that too..."

"So what are you doing to do Baby?"

"Right now... I'm going to chill... with you..." Bazil said as he pulled Trevor into a deep, passionate kiss...

"Baby... what happened?"

"I don't want to talk about it..."

"Tell me..." Trevor pleaded.

"Alright... but I'm thirsty," Bazil said as they both sat up...

"I'll go make us something," Trevor said as he went into the kitchen... Bazil got himself dressed, went into the dining room, and sat at the table...

"What's this?" Bazil said as Trevor came to the table with two plates...

"I thought you might be hungry..." Trevor said as he put the two plates of lasagna with garlic bread on the table...

"As a matter of fact... I am..." Bazil said.

"I'll be back with the wine..." Trevor said as he went back into the kitchen. When he came back to the table, he put the bottle on the table, sat down with Bazil, and took his hand...

"Talk to me..." Trevor said as Bazil began to eat...

"This is good - thank you Trevor..."

"Talk to me..." Trevor pleaded as he picked up Bazil's hand... "Baby... what happened to your hand?

"I don't want to talk about it..."

"Did she do this to you?"

"Yeesss..."

"I'm so sorry Baby..." Trevor said as he began eating...

"It's not your fault..." Bazil sighed... "It's mine..."

"Don't say that..."

"Listen to me Trevor..."

"Okay Baby..."

"She's not like anyone I've ever met before... that's why I asked her to marry me... she's the one Trevor..." Bazil said with tears in his eyes...

"I know she is Baby..." Trevor acknowledged...

"I knew she was hurt... but I saw a side of her I never thought I'd see... and..."

"What Baby?"

"It scared me..."

"Damn..."

"I saw that gun tonight Trevor..."

"You saw it? When?"

"When she tried to shoot me..."

"Oh my God! She tried to kill you?"

"I don't think she was trying to kill me... but she definitely wanted to hurt me... and she succeeded..."

"Damn Baby... what happened?"

"When she came into the house she was so nonchalant about sleeping with you... and I was angry..."

"Oh God Baby... what did you do?"

"She tried to leave me... Trevor..."

"Oh God..."

"I threw her into the counter," Bazil said as he broke down crying...

"Bazil! Did you hurt her?"

"I didn't mean to... it just happened..."

"What just happened?"

"She grabbed the knife... I told her she didn't have it in her... but she did... and she stabbed me..."

"Oh my God!"

"I tried to keep her from leaving... she grabbed her gun from her purse... and she shot at me..."

"Damn Baby... I'm sorry..."

"Somebody called the police... and Katina showed up..."

"Oh shit!"

"And Beautiee let her in as if nothing happened…"

"Damn Baby… what are you going to do?"

"I fucked up Trevor…"

"No you didn't Baby…"

"What if I've lost her? I can't lose her Trevor," he cried.

"You haven't lost her Baby… you've met your match…"

"What?"

"If she were going to leave you she would've left already…"

"You think so Trevor?"

"I know so…"

"What makes you so sure?"

"Bazil Osgood – you are so smart… but so dumb…" Trevor laughed.

"What the fuck Trevor?"

"She loves you just as much as you love her."

"She hates me Trevor."

"Earlier tonight you were so angry you tried to kill me…"

"I'm sorry Trevor."

"You've finally met your equal."

"I didn't think she had it in her…"

"Well… now you know better…"

"I hope I can fix it…"

"You can Baby…"

"I can't lose her Trevor… I just can't…"

"Go home and tell her that…"

"What if she doesn't want me anymore?"

"I'm the one she doesn't want Baby..."

"You're right..."

"Bazil... go get your wife..."

"Okay, okay..." Bazil laughed. "Thank you Trevor," Bazil said as they embraced.

"You're welcome Baby..."

"Oh... Trevor?"

"Yes Baby?"

"I love you..."

"I love you too Baby," Trevor said as Bazil left.

# Chapter 9

"Beautiee... I'm home," Bazil yelled as he came inside, hung up his jacket, and went into the living room... "Beautiee... where are you?" Bazil called as he went into the kitchen and found my letter on the counter...

"Hey my Thirst Quencher," Bazil read as he picked up the letter... "I'm sorry I hurt you. I love you so much and if I had to marry you all over again, I would. When I married you, I promised you I'd love you forever... and I will... but I can't get that image of you and Trevor out of my head. I thought I'd feel better after having sex with Trevor but to be honest, I feel like shit. I had sex with Trevor to hurt you because when I saw you with him it broke my heart – because I know you love him too – and I don't know if I can share you or your heart with anyone else. When you asked me to marry you, you promised me you'd make me feel good every day for the rest of my life – and you broke that promise."

"Beautiee... I'm so sorry..." Bazil said out loud as he broke down crying...

"I'm back home. Please give me time. I'll call you when I'm ready. Love, Beautiee."

"This can't be happening..." Bazil cried as he picked up the phone to call Trevor...

"Hey Baby," Trevor answered...

"She's gone," Bazil whispered.

"She left you?"

"She left me Trevor," he said as he broke down crying again...

"I'm sorry Baby... you want me to come over?"

"That's what got me into this shit in the first place..."

"You're right Baby... I'm sorry... you wanna come back here?"

"No Trevor... I'll call you later..."

"Damn... I never thought I'd be back here," I said out loud as I closed the door and locked it. "Let me check my phone..."

"You have no new messages."

"Good thing I didn't turn off the cable... I need a dose of reality TV," I said out loud as I plopped down on the couch... "Let's see... Monday night... Hmmmmm... Love & Hip Hop should be on," I said out loud as I turned on the TV. After flicking through the channels, I got bored, and went into the kitchen... "Where's my wine... Ohhh... Thank God," I said out loud as I poured myself a glass of wine, picked up the bottle, and sat back down on the couch. I started drinking from the glass and picked up the bottle... "Damn Bazil... all I wanted was some wine... why couldn't you just let me get a glass of wine?" I said as I curled up into a ball and cried like a baby.

# Chapter 10

"Good morning Mrs. Osgood," Sonia said as I came to the window.

"Good morning."

"What can I do for you today?"

"I need to transfer $2,000 into this account," I replied as I gave her a transfer slip."

"Is you husband okay with this transfer?"

"Is my name on the account?"

"Yes it is Mrs. Osgood."

"Well then... I guess it's okay isn't it?" I snapped...

"I'm sorry..."

"I'm sorry Sonia... I know you're just doing your job... I'm just not having a good day," I said as tears started streaming down my face.

"Come inside Mrs. Osgood," Sonia said as she got up from behind the teller window, put her arm around me, and handed me tissues. "Would you like some coffee?" she asked as she sat down beside me...

"Actually... I'd like something stronger," I sniffed.

"Well... I can take an early lunch and we can go to Fridays if you like... it's always happy hour over there," she laughed.

"That's nice of you... but it isn't necessary..."

"Nonsense Mrs. Osgood... I'll take care of your transfer request... and then we're going to lunch," she said as we left her office. "You're all set Mrs. Osgood... let's go," she ordered by waving her hand towards the door as she held it open...

"I don't want you to get in any trouble..."

"I can do anything I need to do to keep Mr. Osgood happy," she laughed. I couldn't hold it in any longer...

"Mrs. Osgood... c'mon... let's get you that drink," she said as she hurried me across the street to Fridays... "Hold on a minute... Yes Mr. Cochran... I'm with Mrs. Osgood... okay... that's fine..." she said as she hung up.

"Good morning, my name is Latasha and I'll be your server... how may I help you?"

"I'll have a Long Island Ice Tea," I answered.

"Isn't it a little early for that?" Latasha laughed. Sonia looked at me pleading for me not to curse Latasha out but she had nothing to worry about...

"Hell no it isn't too early – it's always 5 o'clock somewhere!" I laughed.

"I'll have an Irish coffee," Sonia said.

"I'll be right back with your drinks ladies," Latasha said as she walked away.

"Mrs. Osgood... I don't mean to pry... but you seemed visibly upset..."

"I don't know where to start," I said as I started crying again...

"Start anywhere you like," Sonia said as she touched my hand...

"Bazil cheated on me," I whispered.

"Figures," she sighed.

"It figures?"

"This is why I don't deal with men..."

"What do you mean?"

"I only deal with women Mrs. Osgood."

"Are you a lesbian?"

"Yes I am... by choice... not by birth..."

"Why?"

"Mrs. Osgood... I love men... but as much as they love you... they always hurt you... they can't help it... it's in their nature... they're just built that way.."

"I love him so much," I whispered as I started crying again...

"He loves you too Mrs. Osgood... he's just a man..."

"What did I do wrong?" I sniffed.

"Nothing Mrs. Osgood... it isn't about you... it's about him..."

"It's about him alright," I said as I took a gulp of my Long Island Ice Tea as soon as Latasha placed the drinks on the table.

"That's right Honey," Sonia agreed as she sipped her coffee.

"Will there be anything else ladies?" Latasha asked.

"No thank you," Sonia answered... "I watched my father cheat on my mother over and over again as I was growing up," Sonia said.

"Really?"

"My mother would sit and cry, walk around depressed, and put him out... just to turn around and take him back!" Sonia snapped. "I got tired of it and I swore on my life that no man would ever put me through that shit!" she said as she banged on the table...

"So... you're a virgin?"

"To men... yes... to The Extreme... no," she laughed.

"The Extreme?"

"My dildo," she laughed.

"Oh my God!"

"Oh please Mrs. Osgood... don't act like you've never used one..."

"I haven't..."

"Oh so you've never masturbated?"

"I never said that," I laughed as I finished my drink...

"Would you ladies like refills?" Latasha asked...

"Hell yea!" I laughed as I began feeling my drink...

"Feeling better?" Sonia asked...

"No... not really," I answered as Latasha brought us our drinks...

"Well... I can't tell you what to do... but if it were me... I wouldn't tolerate it," Sonia said as she sipped her coffee...

"I didn't tolerate it... that's why I needed some money transferred this morning..."

"My Girl! That's what I'm talking about... shit... you need me to transfer some more?"

"No... I just needed enough to cover the mortgage..."

"Mr. Osgood has you paying his mortgage?"

"Not his mortgage... mine..."

"Yours? You mean you have your own house?"

"Damn right I do!" I said as I slammed my hand on the table.

"Are you going to leave him?"

"I already did..."

"Yes Honey! I wish my mom would've had your strength..."

"Don't be so hard on your mom Sonia," I said.

"Why not?"

"Because I'm more like your mother than you realize..."

"Damn Mrs. Osgood... is the dick that good?"

"To be honest... yes..."

"Mrs. Osgood... please tell me that's not all there is to it..."

"Sonia... I wish I could make you understand..."

"Try... I'm listening..."

"I've never felt this way about any other man... that's why I married him as soon as I did... he saved my life... and I couldn't let him go... and I didn't want to... and even though he cheated on my with Trevor... I still can't..."

"What did you just say?"

"Ooopppsss..."

"Mr. Osgood cheated on you... with a man?"

"Yes..."

"I don't get it... why do you still want him?"

"Because I do..."

"You're better than me... I would a killed a mutha fucka..."

"I almost did..."

"What? When?"

"Last night..."

"Mrs. Osgood... What happened?"

"We got into a fight..."

"Because he cheated on you?"

"No... because I got revenge..."

"Now that's what I'm talkin' about!" Sonia yelled as she banged her fist on the table... "Was it somebody he knew?"

"Yes..."

"I'm starting to like you a lot Mrs. Osgood... who was it? Was it his best friend?"

"Actually... Trevor is his best friend..."

"What!?"

"Ssshhh... keep your voice down!"

"Wait... wait... wait... you and your husband fucked the same man?"

"Yes..."

"Damn Mrs. Osgood... this could be a fuckin' movie..."

"I know..."

"So wait a minute... you got into a fight... because you fucked his man?"

"That's part of it..."

"Girl... don't stop now... tell me..."

"He wouldn't let me leave..."

"Oooohhh... now I get it... see... typical male bullshit... I'm glad you left..."

"I'm glad I left too... but I'm miserable without him..."

"I still don't understand how you could want him after all this... but hey... the heart wants what the heart wants... at least that's why my mother used to say..."

"I know how your mother feels..."

"I guess you do..."

"Can I ask you a personal question?"

"More personal than what I just told you?"

"You have a point," Sonia laughed...

"Sure," I said.

"Was it good?"

"Was what good?"

"Trevor..."

"He's alright... but he ain't Bazil!" I laughed.

"Oh shit! So you fucked him for nothing?"

"Not really…"

"So…"

"Why'd I do it?"

"Yea…"

"I did it to hurt Bazil…"

"And now you feel like shit…"

"Exactly…"

"Can I ask you another question?"

"Sure…"

"Have you ever been with a woman?"

"Not intimately… why?"

"Well… have you ever thought about it?"

"Honestly?"

"Yes…"

"I'm strictly dickly," I laughed, "but I've had my curiosity peaked once or twice…"

"By anyone in particular?"

"By porn," I laughed.

"Well… if you're interested… I can make you feel better…"

"I don't know Sonia…"

"Having a sexual experience with a woman doesn't turn you into a lesbian… but it will broaden your horizon… and your pleasure," she laughed.

"We'll see about that," I said as I took her face in my hands and kissed her.

"Mrs. Osgood… I wasn't expecting that," she blushed.

"Neither was I," I smiled.

"Here's my number..." Sonia said as she wrote her number down on a napkin and slipped it to me...

"Okay," I squealed. I couldn't believe I was actually entertaining going through with this... "I feel like I'm back in high school and my crush just gave me his phone number," I giggled.

"Shoot... there goes my phone... let me get back to the bank... call me later..." Sonia said as she paid the check and hurried out...

# Chapter 11

"Hey Trevor," Bazil said as he answered the phone.

"Hey Baby…"

"To what do I owe the pleasure?"

"Well… I saw Beautiee earlier today…"

"How'd she look?" Bazil perked up…

"She actually looked happy…"

"She did?"

"Yes she did…"

"Where did you see her?"

"I saw her at Fridays having drinks… she was very happy…"

"She was drunk," Bazil laughed.

"Well… she was with someone and they we're laughing and talking like old friends…"

"Oh that's nice… that makes me happy…"

"You might not be so happy when you find out who she was with…"

"Who was she with?"

"She was with Sonia…"

"My account manager?"

"Yes Bazil…"

"Hmmmmm… I wonder what she's up to? And why was she having drinks with Beautiee?"

"Bazil?"

"Yes Trevor?"

"Did you have Beautiee sign a pre-nuptial agreement?"

"No Trevor..."

"Did you add her to any of your accounts?"

"All of them..."

"Bazil! What the hell's a matter with you?"

"I love her Trevor..."

"You loved the other ones too Bazil – and you never gave them access to anything..."

"I know..."

"Bazil?"

"Yes Trevor?"

"Please check your accounts..."

"Okay... but I know I don't have anything to worry about... I hope..." he said as he turned on his laptop... "Trevor?"

"Yes Bazil?"

"Le'me call you back..."


"Mrs. Osgood! How are you?" Sonia joyfully answered.

"How did you know it was me?"

"I don't give my personal cell number to just anyone," she laughed.

"Well... I was calling..."

"Yes Mrs. Osgood?"

"About what happened earlier today..."

"Yes?"

"Thanks for treating me... I needed that..."

"It was my pleasure Mrs. Osgood..."

"Beautiee..."

"Excuse me?"

"Please... call me Beautiee..."

"Very well Mrs. Osgood... I mean Beautiee... I'm sorry," Sonia laughed.

"That's okay... if you're more comfortable calling me Mrs. Osgood that's fine... in public..."

"Oooohhh... are you suggesting we'll be meeting in private?"

"Yes... I am..."

"I can't wait to see you... Beautiee..."

"I'm looking forward to it... what time is good for you?"

"I'll be home at around 7... how about 7:30?"

"Okay... I'll see you at 7:30..."

"Okay Beautiee... I'll text you my address...

"What are you up to my Beautiee?" Bazil asked out loud as he checked his accounts... "Hmmmmm... I see you transferred $2,000... now what did you do with that money..."

"Bank of America... Marlowe Cochran speaking... How may I help you?"

"Hello Mr. Cochran..."

"Mr. Osgood! What can I do for you?"

"I noticed a transfer of $2,000 from one of my accounts..."

"Hold on... yes... your wife requested the transfer this morning... is there a problem?"

"Not at all Mr. Cochran... I just need to verify which account the money was transferred to..."

"Hold on... UMmmmm... Mr. Osgood?"

"Yes Mr. Cochran?"

"The money was transferred to your wife's account..."

"Hmmmmm... okay... is the money still there?"

"Mr. Osgood... you don't have access..."

"I don't understand..."

"Your wife needs to grant you access or give us permission to discuss account information with you..."

"I'll give my wife a call and get that taken care of..."

"Will there be anything else?"

"No Mr. Cochran... Thank you..."

"You're welcome Mr. Osgood..."

"Okay Beautiee... Let's see what else you've been up to..." Bazil said out loud as he checked his Black American Express account... "I see you've been to the salon... I love it when you get your hair done... Oooohhh... you also went to the spa... That's okay Beautiee... you deserve a day of pampering... whatever you need... I'll see you soon..."

"Yes Mr. Cochran?" Bazil said as he answered his cell...

"Mr. Osgood?"

"Yes?"

"As I said earlier... I can't give you any information about your wife's account... but due to the nature of our relationship I wanted to alert you to something..."

"What's that?"

"The $2,000 was transferred out of your wife's account shortly after it went in..."

"It was?"

"Yes... I'm going to call your wife to make sure no fraud was committed..."

"Okay... Thank you Mr. Cochran..."


"Make yourself comfortable," Sonia said as she opened the door and invited me in.

"Thank you," I said as I sat down on the couch and she handed me a glass of moscato.

"How did you know I liked moscato?"

"You're a sweet person," she laughed.

"I bet you say that to all the girls," I laughed.

"Actually... no..."

"Oh... so I'm not sweet then?"

"Yes Beautiee... you're very sweet," she said as she went back towards the kitchen. I got up off the couch and walked towards the window. The views of the Long Island Sound were breathtaking and relaxing. "Are you ready to eat?" Sonia asked as she came up beside me, wrapping her arm around my waist cautiously...

"UMmmmm..."

"Dinner," she laughed.

"I'm sorry..." I laughed, "It's just when you asked if I was ready to eat..."

"I know..." she laughed.

"What's for dinner?" I asked.

"See for yourself," she answered as she guided me to the dining room...

"Wow," I whispered.

"I wanted tonight to be special." There was a full bottle of moscato, a complete meatloaf dinner from Boston market complete with stuffing, macaroni & cheese, green beans, sweet potato casserole, and cornbread.

"Boston Market," I sighed.

"If you don't like Boston market, I can get something else..."

"I love Boston Market... and I love their meatloaf!" I exclaimed as I sat down at the table. Sonia sat down next to me and I watched her make plates without saying anything...

"You're quiet..."

"I know..."

"Having second thoughts?"

"Hundreds..." I laughed nervously.

"Let's eat," she said as she sat down. As we ate, I admired her in the candlelight. She caught me looking at her and smiled. I finished eating before she did, got up from the table, and started packing things to throw out...

"Beautiee?"

"Yes?"

"Relax..." she said as she touched my hand.

"Let's go out on the deck," I suggested.

"Okay..." she agreed. When we got out on the deck she pulled me close to her and faced me, waiting for me to give her permission to kiss me, and as I leaned in to kiss her, I gave her permission to fully embrace me as well... "I've been dying to kiss you since you kissed me at lunch," she breathed...

"Don't die on me," I laughed as I opened my mouth to kiss her fully...

"Damn Beautiee... you're a great kisser..."

"So are you..." I breathed.

"Let's take this inside..." she breathed.

"Let's not..." I breathed.

"You mean... you want to stay out here? On the deck?"

"Yes..." I breathed as I removed her sweater... "If that's okay with you..."

"Okay..."

"You're so soft..." I breathed as I lifted her arms, pulled her shirt over her head, and pulled her back into a kiss...

"Beautiee..."

"Yes?"

"Wait..."

"Okay..." I said as I stepped back away from her...

"I can't get your blouse off," she said as she began unbuttoning my blouse. Once she unbuttoned it completely she slid my blouse off my shoulders and pulled me back into a full kiss...

"Mmmmmm... you feel so good," I moaned as my hands traveled down her back...

"So do you..." she breathed as she massaged my back with her hands...

"Let me look at you..." I breathed as I stood back from her. I looked at her briefly, then unclasped her bra and exposed her voluptuous breasts with large chocolate nipples... "My God Sonia... you're so beautiful..." I whispered as I began massaging both breasts simultaneously...

"Oh Beautiee... where did you get those hands..." she breathed as I stopped massaging her breasts, took one in my mouth, and started sucking... "Oh Beautiee..." she moaned as I fed on her breasts, first one and then the other, until she stopped me...

"What's wrong?"

"Nothing..." she answered as she unclasped my bra, exposed my c-cups, and began massaging them... "Your breasts are lovely..." she said as she came closer, took my left breast in her mouth, and started swirling her tongue around my nipple...

"Mmmmmm.... I like that..." I breathed as she switched to the right one... "C'mere..." I breathed as I pulled her into a deep kiss, deliberately pressing myself against her and holding her so we could feel each other...

"I've never done this before..." she breathed...

"Neither have I..." I breathed. We continued kissing until Sonia stopped kissing me in my mouth and started kissing me down my body... "Sonia..." I whispered as she loosened my pants and slid them off of me along with my panties...

"Don't move..." she commanded... but I ignored her command, stepping towards her, loosening her pants, and sliding them off of her along with her panties as she did me. Before she could say anything I stepped out of my clothes and pulled her towards me as I leaned back on the bannister of the deck... "Mmmmmm...."

"Mmmmmm....." we both moaned simultaneously as we explored each other's mouths with our tongues and held each other close while the moon cast a bright light on our bodies, giving a spectacular view to whoever was on their deck. Thankfully no one could see behind the deck but what Sonia did next gave anyone within earshot a clue as to what was going on...

"Sooonnnniiiiaaaa!" I moaned as she dropped down between my legs, spread my lips, and began licking and slurping... "Oooohhhh..... Oooohhhh..... Oooohhhh....." I moaned as I leaned back against the deck and gently pushed her head down further...

"Mmmmmm...." She moaned as she pushed my legs apart, slid her tongue inside my pussy, and began slurping...

"Ooohhh shit... yeesss... that's it..." I moaned as she continued. My legs began trembling and instinctively she braced herself underneath me, allowing me to place my legs on her shoulders simultaneously and give her fuller access... "Sonia... Sonia... Sonia..." I moaned as she sucked and slurped faster... causing me to ride her face... "Oh shiittt.. I'm cumming!!" I screamed as I threw my head back, grabbed her head, and fucked her face... "Oooohhh shit... don't stop... I'm cumming again... Aaaaagggghhhhh!!" I screamed as Sonia grabbed my ass with both hands and continued sucking and slurping... "Ooohhh... Oooohhh..... Ooohhhh... I'm still cumming!!" I moaned as Sonia began sucking my clit ferociously. Sonia began to slow down as my orgasms subsided but didn't stop right away. I stood there with my eyes closed and enjoyed her mouth and tongue for a while until she spoke...

"You needed that..." she breathed as she stood up in front of me...

"Yesss..." I moaned as I pulled her closer to me and began liking my juices off her mouth while sucking her lips...

"Mmmmmm...." she moaned...

"Mmmmmm... is right..." I breathed as I started kissing her fully in the mouth...

"Let's go inside..." she breathed...

"Let's not..." I breathed in between kisses...

"You ready for round two?"

"We haven't finished round one..." I breathed as I slid myself down between her legs...

"Oh Beautiee..." she moaned as I started licking her lips... it was a bit awkward at first being that I had never done this before, but as I followed her moans, her hands as she guided my head, and her wetness, I brought her down onto the chaise lounge, spread her legs, and dove into her, sending her into a state of orgasmic bliss...

"Mierda, mamá ... eso se siente tan bien ... no te detengas ... allí mismo ... sí ... ¡ya voy! ¡Ya voy! Shit Mommy... that feels so good... don't stop... right there... yes... I'm cumming! I'm cumming!" she screamed as she arched her back and road out her orgasmic wave on my mouth...

"Mmmmmm...." I moaned as I tasted and swallowed every bit of her creaminess...

"Damn Beautiee... you sure you've never done this before?" she breathed...

"Never," I said as I continued to lick her...

"Will you do something for me?" I stopped licking her, lay on top of her, and started kissing her...

"What... would... you ... like..."

"Come... inside... with... me... I'll... show... you..." she breathed...

"Mmmmmm..." I moaned as I kissed her fully... "Okay..." I answered as we picked up our clothes, headed inside, dropped the clothes on the couch, and proceeded to the bedroom...

"Open the drawer..." she commanded as she lay on the bed on her back...

"Okay..." I said as I opened the drawer... and I couldn't believe what I saw... "Oh my God!

What the hell is this?" I asked as I read the tag:
Big Black Extreme...

"Haven't you ever seen a strap on?" she
laughed.

"Yes... but only in porn... what are you up
to?"

"Put it on... please..." she begged.

"Okayyy..." I said as I stepped into the
harness and secured it around me... "So this is
what it's like to have a big black dick," I laughed.

"Come closer Beautiee..." Sonia
commanded as she moved towards the edge of the
bed and grabbed it... "Tell me to suck it..." she
commanded while looking up at me...

"Suck it..." I repeated. I watched in
amazement as she took The Extreme in her
mouth, deep throated it, pulled it out of her
mouth, spit on it, then take it back in her
mouth... and in that moment... I started thinking
of Bazil. She continued sucking on The Extreme
and started moaning... all the while I was
imagining what I would do to Bazil if he were
here...

"Come here Beautiee..." she said as she
patted the bed for me to lie beside her. I lay
beside her and started to kiss her but she
interrupted me... "I want you to fuck me
Beautiee..."

"Ummmmm..."

"Please Beautiee..."

"I don't know how..." I whispered.

"Just ease inside... I'll guide you..."

"Okay..." I said as I climbed on top of her and started easing The Extreme inside her... "You okay?" I asked as I started to kiss her...

"Mmmmmm ... Mami ... fóllame ... Oh, sí ... mamá más dura ... más profundo ... Estoy llegando mamá ... ¡Voy! Mmmmmm...." she said as I started moving in and out of her... "Mommy... fuck me... Oh yes... harder Mommy... deeper..." she moaned as I thrust harder and faster... "I'm cumming Mommy... I'm cumming!" I slowed down but didn't stop until she rode out her orgasm...

"Mmmmmm..." I moaned as I kissed her... "Your face is beautiful when you cum..."

"Let me fuck you Beautiee..." she breathed as we continued kissing...

"No..."

"I wanna make you feel good Beautiee..."

"You already have..."

"Just try it... you'll like it..."

"I said no Sonia," I said as I got up off her, got out the bed, removed the strap-on, and went into the living room to get my clothes. She followed me and sat down beside me...

"I'm sorry... I didn't mean to offend you..."

"Don't be," I said as I kissed her... "I'm not offended... I'm just not fucking anybody but Bazil...

"Oohhh... I see... so you didn't like fucking me?"

"It was weird... but I did like making you cum..."

"I liked it too..."

"I need to get home," I said as I started getting dressed...

"You sure you don't wanna stay?"

"Yea... I'm sure..."

"Can I see you again?"

"Yes..." I said as I pulled her into a kiss... "I'd like that..."

"Can you come back tomorrow?"

"Yes... I'll be back tomorrow..."

"Good..." she said as we both got up and she walked me to the door... "Beautiee?"

"Yes Sonia?" I answered as I turned to face her and she pulled me into a deep kiss. I pulled her closer and continued kissing her deeply...

"Mmmmmm.... Sure you can't stay?"

"I need to go home Sonia... I'll see you tomorrow," I said as I left. I got in a cab and as much as I thought about Sonia... I missed Bazil.

# Chapter 12

It was Friday night. I'd been coming to Sonia's house every night since last Saturday... and I was enjoying it... but as good as Sonia made me feel, she was making me ache for Bazil..."Don't stop... that's it... right there...," I moaned. She was good. She had me squirting like Bazil never did...

"You cummin' Mommy?" she stopped to ask. Instantly I went from orgasmic euphoria to rage. I wanted to smack her good and hard upside her head for stopping right before I was about to explode but more than that I needed to cum so instead of smacking her upside her head I continued to run my fingers through her hair and caress her scalp as I propped myself up to look directly into her eyes.

"I love you Mommy," she whispered as I guided her mouth back to where I needed it to be and gasped when she went back to work. I laid my head back and arched my back just enough for her to slide her hands up under my ass and bury her face deeper while her tongue flicked my clit and fucked my pussy simultaneously...

"Oooohhh..... Oooohhh..... Oooohhh.....," I moaned as the entire lower half of my body trembled and my legs locked around her head. I was riding her face good and hard and with each wave of orgasmic pleasure as my clit suffocated her nose. She continued to flick my clit and fuck my pussy with her tongue softly as my orgasmic euphoria began to descend down my body, sending mini shock waves through me as my breathing returned to normal.

"You okay Mommy?" she asked as I closed my eyes. I didn't answer her. She started kissing her way up my stomach to my breasts, sucking on first the left nipple, then the right. When she got up to my neck, I wrapped my arm around her and pulled her down to hold her. I knew she loved me and even though the feeling wasn't mutual, I could never hurt her while she was this vulnerable. She looked up at me with so much love in her eyes I kissed her on her forehead and pulled her back down close to me so I could hold her some more. After we lay together for a while, I propped myself up to look at her.

"You ready for The Extreme baby?" I asked.

"Yes, Mommy, yes...," she breathed. I pulled her face to mine and began kissing her gently at first, but she was hungry and horny and started sucking my tongue with extreme fervor. I pulled away from her, got up on my knees, reached into the nightstand, and pulled out The Extreme Strap On Dildo we bought from tootimid.com. Her eyes watered as she watched me strap it on. I eased my way on my knees towards her mouth and caressed her hair. She happily obliged and began sucking and slurping on The Extreme, moaning as if she was sucking my real dick. I began to play with her pussy and when I inserted my fingers, she fucked my hand with The Extreme going deeper down her throat. I couldn't for the life of me understand how she got so turned on sucking a dildo instead of a real dick, but hey – this was her fantasy so I let her enjoy it for a while until I saw her creaming in my hand. I pulled my fingers out of her pussy, pulled The Extreme out of her mouth, and replaced The Extreme with my fingers so she could taste herself.

"Turn over," I whispered.

"Yes Mommy," she breathed as she obeyed.

"Get on your knees," I commanded.

"Yes Mommy," she breathed as she got on her knees, grabbed the headboard, and spread her legs. I slapped her ass playfully as I inched the Extreme closer to her pussy.

"Tell Mommy what you want," I whispered as I bent down to her ear while simultaneously rubbing the head of the Extreme up and down her clit.

"Fuck me Mommy," she panted as she spread her legs wider. I could have rammed the Extreme up inside her all the way to the hilt and she would have loved every minute of it but instead I treated her the way I would want to be treated – I eased the Extreme in slowly until I was all the way inside her. "Si Mami si! Yes Mommy, Yyyyeeeessss!" she squealed as she began fucking the Extreme herself without me moving. I grabbed her by her hips to steady myself and began meeting her thrust for thrust, still being as gentle as I could so I wouldn't hurt her, but she let me know I had nothing to worry about... "Sí mami me jodas más duro ya voy! Yes Mommy... Fuck me... harder... I'm cumming..." I stopped and immediately pulled out of her. She got up on her knees, turned to face me, and instead of being angry for stopping before she could cum, she was hurt. I pulled her close to me, pushed her down on the bed, climbed on top of her, and spread her legs.

"You wanna cum for Mommy?" I whispered as I slid the Extreme inside her and began thrusting...

"Si Mami si si si! Yes Mommy... Yes... Yeeesssss!" she screamed as I continued thrusting. I couldn't believe this was what she wanted, but hey – who was I to judge... "Estoy llegando... estoy llegando... Aaaahhhhh! I'm cummin..... I'm cummin..... I'm cummin..... Aaaahhhhhh!" she cried out. I slowed down my momentum and continued thrusting as her orgasmic euphoria began to descend and she started moaning... "Mommy... Mommy... Mommy... Mommy..." I lifted her up as I got on my knees and watched her fuck the Extreme as I held her in place until she collapsed on the bed and I collapsed on top of her, still inside her. I lay there with her for a few moments, and then I got up off her, removed The Extreme, placed it back in the drawer, and went into the living room. Sonia followed behind me and sat down on the couch as she watched me get dressed... "You're leaving aren't you?"

"Yes Sonia."

"I mean... for good..."

"Yes Sonia... for good."

"Why? What did I do?" she asked with tears in her eyes...

"Sonia... c'mere..." I said as I pulled her into a kiss... "You didn't do anything. You're so beautiful... you deserve to be happy... but it can't be with me..."

"Why not? Don't you love me?"

"Sonia... I care about you... more than I've ever cared for any other woman in my life... but I want Bazil..."

"How could you? He'll just hurt you again..."

"I'm willing to take that chance..."

"Why not take a chance with me?"

"Sonia... if I continue to do this with you..."

"You'll be happy... I know you will..."

"Sonia... yes... I'm very happy when I'm with you..."

"So why are you throwing it all away?"

"Sonia... I love Bazil... I want Bazil..."

"So what was this then?"

"This..." I answered as I pulled her into a deep kiss... "Was... a... wonderful.... incredible... exhilarating... experience I'll never forget... but I want Bazil... I need Bazil..."

"Will I ever see you again?"

"The door's open..." I answered as I left. As soon as I got in a cab, I called Bazil. "Oh good – voicemail..." I breathed...

"Beautiee..." Bazil said out loud as he picked up his cell phone and smiled. "Hey my Thirst Quencher," he listened with anticipation and excitement... "I'm glad you didn't answer the phone because I can say what I want to say without you interrupting me with kisses... or anything else. I love you... I miss you... I want you... I need you... I'm coming home... I'll see you later..."

## Punishment

"My Thirst Quencher," I breathed as Bazil pulled me into a deep, passionate kiss...

"Beautiee..." he moaned in between kisses....

"I missed you so much..."

"I missed you too..."

"What's wrong Bazil? Aren't you happy to see me?"

"Very..."

"What's wrong then?"

"You left me Beautiee..."

"You hurt me Bazil..."

"I know... and I'm sorry..." he said as he pushed me away from him... "But you need to be punished..."

"Punished? For what?" I snapped...

"For denying me pussy..."

"Oooohhhh..." I breathed. The thought of being punished turned me on... and Bazil knew it...

"Come with me," Bazil commanded as he took me by the hand and led me upstairs to the bedroom... "Take off your clothes..." Bazil commanded... "Come here to me..." he commanded as he watched me walk towards him... "Undress me... slowly..."

"Yes my Thirst Quencher," I said as I began undressing him. I took my time slidding his shirt off his shoulders and down his arms... "Damn you smell good," I moaned as I began kissing him down his chest...

"Stop..." Bazil commanded... "Go sit on the edge of the bed..."

"Okay!" I squealed. I sat on the bed and watched Bazil come towards me. Once he was standing in front of me he picked my head up by my chin...

"Who am I?"

"My Thirst Quencher..." I breathed. Bazil unbuckled his belt, dropped his pants, and stood before me with his dick directly in front of me...

"Open your mouth..." he commanded as I opened my mouth... "Quench your Thirst..." he commanded as he slowly placed his dick in my mouth... "Yeeesss.... Beautiee..." Bazil moaned as I quenched my thirst... "MmmmMmmmmm..... That's it... suck it..." he moaned as he grabbed me by the head and pushed his dick in deeper... "I'm about to cumm.... Beautiee.... Beautiee..." he moaned as I swallowed him... "Shhiittt.... Fuck.... Fuck... Fuck.... Aaaaaaggghhhh!" He continued to stand there and let me suck his dick for a few moments until he spoke... "I'm not done with you..."

"I know..."

"Lay back... and spread your legs..."

"Yes my Thirst Quencher..." I breathed as I did as I was told...

"Mmmmmm..." he moaned... "Look at my pretty pussy..." he breathed as he slid two fingers inside me, pulled them out, and licked them... "You taste different," he said as he licked his fingers... "Damn you're so wet..." he breathed as he got on his knees, slid his hands under my ass, pulled me to the edge, spread my legs... and dove in...

"Bazil..." I moaned as he began licking, sucking, and slurping...

"Mmmmmm... you taste sweeter than before..." he breathed as he slipped his tongue inside me...

"Oh Bazil..." I moaned as he swirled his tongue inside, then spread my lips and began sucking... "Bazziiiilll!" I screamed as I arched my back and I came in his mouth... "Mmmmmm... you taste so good..." he breathed as he continued licking and sucking... "So... Beautiee... who is she?"

"Whhhaaattt?" I asked as I tried to sit up but Bazil pushed me back down on the bed, continuing to lick and suck...

"Who is she?"

"How did you know?" I breathed as I grabbed his head and pushed him down between my legs...

"Once... a... woman... experiences... an... orgasm... with... another... woman... she...

changes... for... the... better..." he moaned as he picked up the pace...

"Ohhhh.... Bazzziiilll..." I moaned as I started riding his face... "How?"

"There's... something... about... a... woman's... tongue... that... brings... out... the... sweetest... nectar... from... the... pussy..." Bazil moaned as he continued sucking...

"Bazil... Bazil... Bazil..." I moaned as he slid his hands under my ass and buried his head further and his tongue deeper... "Aaaagggghhhh.... Aaaagggghhhh.... Aaaagggghhhh!" I screamed before collapsing on the bed. I watched as Bazil stood up, climbed up on the bed, and lay on top of me...

"Taste yourself," he commanded as he pulled me into a deep kiss, slipping his tongue inside as he covered my mouth complete...

"Mmmmmm......" I moaned as I enjoyed the taste...

"So..." Bazil asked as he slid himself inside me and began thrusting... "Who... is... she?"

"Sonia!" I moaned...

"From... the... bank?"

"Yyyeeessss!" I moaned.

"Did... she... fuck... you?"

"Nooo..... Bazil..." I moaned.

"Did... you... miss... me?"

"Yeeesss! Ooohhh... Bazziilll..."

"You... need... to... be... taught... a... lesson..." Bazil growled as he began thrusting harder and faster...

117

"Bazil... Bazil... Bazzziiilll!" I screamed...

"Yessss Beautiee... who's... pussy... is... this..."

"Yooouuurrrsss!" I screamed as I came again. Bazil continued thrusting until my orgasm subsided and then got up off of me...

"Get up and turn your ass towards me..." he commanded. I did as I was told and as I did I could feel the tip of Bazil's dick on my ass... "Grab the headboard and hold on..." Bazil commanded... "Spread your legs..." Bazil commanded... "May I?" Bazil whispered in my ear as he slipped on a condom and lotioned it with Vaseline. I could feel the tip of his dick on my ass as he laid himself on my back...

"I don't know Bazil..."

"Please Beautiee..." he whispered in my ear as he began playing with my pussy...

"Ooohhh... that feels good..."

"This will too... I promise..."

"Okay..." I breathed... trembling...

"Relax Beautiee... I won't hurt you..." he whispered as he slowly began inserting himself in my ass...

"MmmmMmmm..." I moaned as he continued playing with my pussy while going in further...

"Are you okay?" he asked as he began thrusting...

"Oh Bazil..." I moaned as I began to enjoy sensations from Bazil indirectly hitting my G spot. Bazil stopped playing with my pussy and pulled me close to him, breathing heavy in my ear, still thrusting... "Bazil... I'm gonna cummmm..." I moaned...

"I'm cumming with you Beautiee..." he growled in my ear as he began thrusting deeper...

"Bazil... Bazil... Bazil..."

"Beautiee... Beautiee.... Beautiee...."

"Aaaagggghhhh!" We both collapsed on the bed while Bazil was still inside me... "Beautiee..." he whispered in my ear while kissing my neck...

"Bazil..." I moaned...

"Turn over Beautiee..." Bazil commanded as he slid out my ass, took off the condom, dropped it on the floor, climbed on top of me, pinned my hands above my head with his, spread my legs with his knee, and slid back inside me... "Listen to me Beautiee..." he breathed as he began thrusting...

"Yes my Thirst Quencher..." I moaned as Bazil began kissing me on my neck and earlobe...

"If... you... ever... leave... me... again... I'll... fuck... you... to... death... do... you... understand... me?"

"Yeeessss Bazil.... Yeeessss!" I moaned... "Mmmmmm..... good..."

# Chapter 14

"Good morning..." Bazil said as he woke me up, kissing me and messaging my breasts...

"Yesss... it... is..." I moaned as he moved his hand from my breasts to my body...

"I missed you Beautiee..." he moaned...

"I missed you too..."

"Even though you were with Sonia?" he asked as he propped himself up on his elbow to look down at me while continuing to touch me all over...

"Yeesss..." I moaned, closing my eyes...

"I cried when you left..." he said, tearing up. I opened my eyes and saw his were filling with tears... and so were mine...

"Oh Bazil..." I said as I kissed tears off his face... "I love you sooo much... please don't cry," I said as I started crying too...

"If you stop... I'll stop..." he said as he kissed me fully..."

"I cried too..."

"You did?" he asked with relief in his voice...

"Yes Bazil..."

"I'm sorry Beautiee..." he said as he kissed me and I could feel his tears...

"I'm sorry too..." I said as I started crying...

"You have nothing to be sorry for Beautiee..."

"Yes Bazil... I do..."

"No Beautiee..."

"Bazil... listen to me..."

"Okay..."

"I know it hurt you when I left you... and I'm sorry..."

"I didn't give you a choice..."

"Bazil?"

"Yesss..."

"Can we talk?"

"Okay..." he sighed. "I'll go make breakfast... and coffee..." he said as he got up out of bed. When he reached for his boxers I stopped him...

"Bazil?"

"Yes?"

"Leave your boxers here... it's been a while since I've seen you in all your glory..."

"It's chilly..."

"Put on your robe... but leave it open slightly... so I can enjoy the view..."

"Okay..." he smiled as he put on his robe, leaving it slightly open, and went downstairs to make breakfast. I got up out of bed when I started to smell coffee, put on my robe, and went downstairs to the kitchen...

"Just in time Beautiee..." he said as he handed me a cup of coffee with hazelnut creamer...

"Mmmmm.... I missed this..." I moaned.

"You didn't have coffee?"

"I didn't have your coffee," I said as I pulled him into a kiss. "Mmmmmm..." I moaned as I pulled him to me, slid my hand inside his robe, and grabbed his ass...

"Mmmmmm...." He moaned as my robe fell open and he pressed his dick up against me...

"I need to finish my coffee," I laughed as I stopped.

"Hmmmm.... alright," he said as he sat down at the table with a cup of coffee for himself...

"Can I ask you something Bazil?"

"Sure."

"Have you always... you know..."

"Am I gay?"

"Yes."

"No..."

"I'm confused..."

"Let me explain..."

"Okay..."

"As I told you, I met Trevor in prison and we hit it off..."

"Okay..."

"I was good for a while... but..."

"It's okay Bazil... tell me..." I said as I got up from the table, walked over to him, and put my arm around him...

"I don't want to hurt you Beautiee..."

"I know Bazil... it's okay..."

"One night I was jacking off... and... he caught me..."

"Oooohhh..."

"I didn't realize he was watching... I was embarrassed..."

"I would be too..."

"He offered to suck my dick... and I got angry at him for even suggesting it... but it had been so long... I'd never been with a man... I'd never thought about being with a man... he suggested I close my eyes and pretend he was a woman... so I did... and I enjoyed it..."

"I understand Bazil..."

"How can you understand it Beautiee? I don't even understand it..."

"You're a man... you have needs..."

"It went like that for a while... but one night I started talking about how much I missed getting pussy..."

"And he asked you to fuck him," I sighed...

"Yea... I kept telling myself I wasn't gay - 'cause I'm not - I was just getting' some ass and bustin' a nut..."

"But you caught feelings..."

"Yea... I know I shouldn't have... but I did... I tried not too..."

"You love him don't you?"

"Yes Beautiee..." he whispered with tears in his eyes...

"Why me?"

"I always wanted to get married... like I said... I'm not gay..."

"How does Trevor feel about that?"

"He hates it... but I'll never be that for him... especially now that I have you..."

"Bazil?"

"Yes Beautiee?"

"We're you ever going to tell me about him?"

"Yes Beautiee..."

"What you did was selfish..."

"I know..."

"You made me love you so I couldn't leave... even if I wanted to..."

"I know... I'm sorry..."

"I know you are... but I have to be honest..."

"Yes Beautiee?"

"I can't lose you," I said with tears in my eyes..."

"Oh Beautiee..." Bazil cried as he pulled me into a kiss... "Never... I promise..." he cried as he kissed me again and again... "I'll tell him it's over...

"You will?"

"Yes Beautiee..."

"Oh Bazil..." I cried harder... "I love you sooo much..."

"I love you too..."

"Are you sure? I know you love him..."

"Yes... I do love him... but you're my wife... I hurt you... you came back to me... and you still want me... I love you..." he cried as he pulled me into a kiss..."

"Stop Bazil..."

"What's wrong?"

"I need to tell you something..."

"Okay..."

"I went to fuck him to hurt you..."

"I know..."

"I'm sorry..."

"Can I ask you something Beautiee?"

"Yes..."

"Did you... umm..."

"Hell no!" I saw the relief on Bazil's face but I didn't say anything...

"I went to see Trevor after Katina left..."

"Did you fuck him?" Bazil didn't bother to answer... he just turned his head away from me... "Bazil?"

"Yes Beautiee?"

"Why was Katina here?"

"We fought."

"Bazil?"

"Yes Beautiee?"

"Why was Katina here?"

"Katina is a detective from the Special Investigations Unit in Milford, Connecticut. She was the detective who arrested me...Beautiee?"

"Yes Bazil?"

"Was Sonia your first?"

"Yes."

"What made you... you know..."

"I told her what happened between us..."

"Why?"

"I went to transfer money... we exchanged words... one thing led to another... I started crying... she brought me into her office and offered me coffee but I said I wanted something stronger... then she took me out for drinks..."

"I'm sorry Beautiee..."

"I know..."

"So how did... you know..."

"We started drinking... and talking... she told me that's why she's never been with a man and she only deals with women..."

"Really?"

"Yes..."

"So how did you..."

"She asked me if I had ever been with a woman... I told her I hadn't but I was curious... she said if I was interested she might be able to make me feel better... so I kissed her..."

"Oh my..." Bazil breathed... I could tell this was exciting him... especially when he got up from the table, came over to me, pulled me up, turned me around, moved my robe, and bent me over... "Did she eat you?" he breathed as he slid inside me and started thrusting..."

"Yeeesss..." I moaned as I spread my legs and grabbed the table...

"Where did you do it?"

"On her deck..." I moaned...

"Did you cum?"

"Oh yesss..." I moaned...

"How many times did you cum?"

"Three..." I moaned...

"Did you eat her too?" he asked as he thrust harder...

"Yeessss..." I moaned...

"Did you make her come?"

"Yeesss! Yeesss!" I moaned...

"Did you enjoy it?"

"Yes Bazil... Yeessss!" I screamed as I came... but he wasn't finished...

"I want you to invite her over... so I can watch..." he breathed as he pulled me closer and whispered in my ear as he continued thrusting... "I want to watch you come!" he growled...

"Oh Bazil!" I moaned...

"Cum for me again!" he growled as he thrust harder and deeper...

"Baaazzziiilll!" I screamed as my legs trembled...

"MmmmMmmmph... MmmmMmmmph... MmmmMmmmph! Oh shiiittt... I'm cummin... Aaaaggghhh!" he continued thrusting... slowing his pace, but not stopping... I want to watch her make you cum," he breathed as he turned me around, pulled me to him, and kissed me deeply...

"Yes my Thirst Quencher... yes..." I breathed as we slowly stopped kissing...

"Sit down... I'll make breakfast now..." he breathed as he took the food out of the fridge... "So... how long did it last?" Bazil asked as he scrambled the eggs for the omelet...

"How many days was I gone?"

"About a week..."

"That long…"

"So… did you spend the night?"

"No."

"Why not?" Bazil asked as he put the turkey bacon in the frying pan…

"I didn't want to… I wanted to go home…"

"There's something you're not telling me…"

"Yes…"

"Did something happen Beautiee?" he asked as he came over to me and put his arm around me…

"Yea…"

"What happened?"

"Bazil… I never wanted to spend the night… I wanted to go home…"

"Damn…" Bazil laughed as he went to take the bacon out of the pan and start cooking the omelets… "You just wanted to bust a nut and bounce…"

"Yea…"

"I still don't understand why you never spent the night…"

"What does it matter?"

"I'm sorry… I'll stop asking…" he said as he put the bacon and omelets on plates, got forks, brought them to the table, and asked again… "What happened?"

"I don't know if I should tell you…" I said as I started eating…

"Oh yes… yes you should… please…"

"She had a dildo…"

"Nothing weird about that…"

"It was a strap on..."

"Oooohhh... this is getting juicy... tell me more..." he salivated as he finished his food...

"I put it on..." I said as I finished eating... "And..."

"And?" Bazil asked.

"She started sucking it..."

"Oh Shit!"

"She told me to tell her to suck it..."

"Damn! This is better than porn! Did you do it?"

"Yea..."

"You didn't like controlling her?"

"I started thinking about you..."

"You did?"

"Yea..."

"That's sweet," he said as he leaned in to kiss me...

"I don't know why, but when I saw her sucking the dildo... all I could think about was sucking you..."

"Aww..." he said as he rubbed my back...

"Then she asked me to fuck her..."

"Ooohhhh shiittt!"

"I liked knowing I turned her on... and things were going good... until she wanted to fuck me with it..."

"Ohhh shit! She fucked you too?"

"Hell no!"

"You didn't want her to?"

"Bazil?"

"Yes Beautiee?"

"If I wanted to get fucked by a dildo... I'd ask my husband to do it..." I said as I pulled him into a kiss...

"Aww... I love you Beautiee..."

"I love you too..." I said as we continued kissing for a few minutes... "There's something else..."

"What?"

"The dildo is your complexion... and it had a name..."

"Aaaahhhaaaaa..... Aaaahhhhaaaa... Aaaahhhaaaa... what's the name?

"The Extreme..."

"So... you didn't enjoy being with her?"

"Yes... she made me feel good... and she felt good too..."

"What was it like when you... ate her pussy... did you like it?'

"Yes... I liked it... a lot..."

"I see..." he said as he rubbed his chin in thought...

"She spoke Spanish then too..."

"Damn Beautiee... she thought she was turning you out but you ended up turning her out," he laughed.

"You're right," I laughed. "She kept asking me if I was sure I've never done it before..."

"Have you?"

"No Bazil..."

"Beautiee?"

"Yes Bazil?"

"What did you do with the money?"

"I paid my mortgage..."

"Beautiee?"

"Yes Bazil?"

"Have you ever thought about selling your house?"

"Yea..."

"Maybe we can discuss it with Mr. Cochran... when you're ready..."

"Okay..." I said as I drifted off...

"Beautiee? Beautiee?"

"Oh... sorry... I was just thinking..."

"About what?"

"About Sonia..." I sighed.

"I can't wait to watch you..." Bazil breathed.

"I hope she's willing..."

"She won't give you any trouble..."

"What makes you so sure?"

"She's feeling you... big time..."

"Naaa..."

"Trust me Beautiee... she's feeling you..."

"Okay... if you say so..." I said as I got up from the table and yawned... "I'm going back to bed..."

"I know so..." Bazil said as he followed me back upstairs...

# Chapter 15

"Good morning Mr. Osgood," Sonia said with a smile as Bazil walked into the bank.

"Good morning," Bazil replied, eyeing her mischievously...

"What can I do for you today?"

"HMmmmm... well... since you asked... let's take this somewhere private," Bazil said as he walked behind the counter...

"Mr. Osgood!" Mr. Cochran said with a smile... "How's everything?"

"Everything's fine," Bazil answered.

"Sonia, are you taking care of Mr. Osgood personally?"

"Yes Marlowe... I mean Mr. Cochran..." she stuttered...

"It's okay Sonia... you can call me Marlowe in front of Mr. Osgood..."

"Yes sir... Marlowe..." she stuttered again..

"Sonia... I need to go over one of my accounts with you..." Bazil reminded, making Sonia feel uneasy...

"Is there something wrong Mr. Osgood?" Sonia asked, pleading for Bazil not to take her in her office with her eyes...

"We need to discuss this in private," Bazil answered, changing his tone to let Sonia know he was serious...

"Oh... Okay Mr. Osgood... come with me..." she said as he followed her into the office and closed the door...

"Lock the door..." Bazil commanded.

"Please Bazil... don't make me do this... not here..." she said with tears in her eyes...

"Sonia..." he breathed as he pulled her close to him and began kissing her on her neck...

"Please don't..." she whispered as Bazil continued kissing her on her neck...

"You disappoint me Sonia..." Bazil whispered in her ear as he continued to hold her close...

"I'm sorry... I didn't mean to..."

"Now now..." he whispered in her ear as he sucked her neck a little... "Don't lie to me..."

"Okay... I'll tell you the truth... please let me go..."

"Not yet... I'm enjoying this..."

"Please Bazil... you're scaring me..."

"I know..." Bazil said as he began rubbing her back while nuzzling her neck..."

"Please don't do this..." she whispered as she began to cry...

"Look at me Sonia..." Bazil commanded...

"Yes Bazil?" she said as she looked directly at Bazil... trembling...

"Stop crying," he said as he began kissing her tears off her face...

"Okay..." she said as she leaned in to kiss him. Bazil pulled her into a full embrace and held her while kissing her deeply for a few minutes before letting her go... "That was nice..." she breathed in relief as she sat down. Bazil sat beside her.

"My wife told me everything..."

"I know..."

"How do you know?"

"I just do..."

"We had a deal Sonia..."

"I know..."

"It's time to pay what you owe..."

"I know... but not here... please... I'm begging you..."

"Shhhhh!" Bazil said as he pulled Sonia into a kiss... "In all the years you've known me... have I ever hurt you?"

"Nooo..."

"So why would I hurt you now?"

"I guess you wouldn't..."

"You guess? You're not sure?"

"I don't know Bazil..." she whispered...

"Sonia... I'm not here to hurt you... I would never hurt you... I promise..."

"You promise?"

"Yes... now relax..."

"Okay... I'll try..."

"As I said... we had a deal..."

"I know..."

"And... I'm here to collect..."

"Okay..." she said as she started unbuttoning her blouse...

"Sonia... stop..."

"But you said..."

"Sonia... not here..."

"Oh thank God..." she breathed as she fixed her blouse...

"I want you to come to my home... and I want you to make love to my wife... and I want to watch..."

"Really?"

"Yes... and then... you'll let me make love to you..." he said as he pulled her into a kiss...

"What if I don't want to?"

"What if you do?" Bazil said as he continued to kiss her...

"Why do you do this?"

"Do what?"

"Why do you bother to deal with women at all when all you do is hurt them? You're no better than my father!" she snapped.

"I'm nothing like your father Sonia..."

"Yes you are! You go from woman to woman and keep your boyfriend on the side – and you never try to change – and when it doesn't work out you just find another one! When will it end Bazil?"

"Your memory is very selective I see..." Bazil said as he grabbed Sonia. When she tried to pull away he pulled her closer... close enough for her to see a side of him she hasn't seen in a long time... "You had no problem with me when you needed my help with your father... did you Sonia?" he growled...

"No... Bazil... I didn't..."

"You had no problem with me when you needed this job... did you Sonia?"

"No... Bazil... I didn't..."

"And..." Bazil said as he grabbed her by the back of her neck and began kissing her... "You... had... no... problem... with... any... of... the... women... I... found... in fact... you've... gotten... a... lot... more... pussy... since... you've... met... me... isn't... that... right... Sonia?"

"Yyyyeeeesssss...." Sonia stuttered...

"So... just... so... we're... clear... you... don't... have... a... problem... now... do... you?"

"No... Bazil..."

"Good..." Bazil said as he stopped kissing her... "Now tell me... did you enjoy making love to my wife?" he asked as he slid his hand between her legs...

"Yes... Bazil..." she moaned as he slid his hand in her panties...

"Did she make you cum?" Bazil asked as he started playing with her pussy...

"Yes... Bazil..." she moaned as she spread her legs allowing him further access...

"What did her pussy taste like?" Bazil asked as he pulled her closer, inserting two fingers in her pussy...

"Her pussy was sweet Bazil," she moaned as she lay back on the couch, closed her eyes, and soaked Bazil's hand with her juices...

"Cum for me..." Bazil breathed in her ear as he pushed his fingers in deeper, massaging her G spot...

"Bazil... Bazil..." Sonia moaned as she grabbed Bazil's hand to push his fingers in further... and Bazil stopped abruptly... "Why did you stop?" she breathed...

"Patience Sonia," Bazil said as he pulled his hand out her panties, licked his fingers, and stood up to leave... "We wouldn't want to do anything too Extreme..." he said as he left the office and closed the door...

# Chapter 16

"Hey Baby," Trevor said as he opened the door... "I missed you," Trevor said as he pulled Bazil into a kiss...

"Trevor..."

"Yes Baby?" Trevor breathed as he attempted to kiss Bazil again...

"We need to talk..." Bazil said as he went to sit in the living room. Trevor followed Bazil and sat beside him on the sofa.

"How's things with Beautiee?" Trevor asked, dreading the answer...

"Things couldn't be better..." Bazil answered looking away...

"Bazil... Baby... please don't do this..." Trevor said as he started to cry...

"I'm sorry Trevor..." Bazil said as he started to cry too... "We can't do this anymore..."

"Why? Haven't I always been there for you?"

"Yes Trevor... you have..."

"Then why?"

"Because I love her..." Bazil answered, still crying...

"You said you love me too!" Trevor cried.

"I do love you Trevor... I'll probably always love you..."

"Probably? What the fuck does that even mean?"

"Trevor... I do love you... but I'm choosing Beautiee..." he said as he attempted to touch Trevor on his shoulder...

"Don't you dare touch me!" Trevor screamed. "How could you do this to me after everything I've done for you?"

"Trevor... this isn't about you... it's about Beautiee..."

"Fuck Beautiee!" Trevor screamed... and then he looked at Bazil in terror as Bazil grabbed him by the throat...

"Don't EVER speak about my wife that way again... are we clear?" Trevor nodded his head in agreement as Bazil loosened his grip around Trevor's throat... "I love you Trevor..." Bazil said as he pulled Trevor into a kiss and Trevor embraced him...

"Please don't leave me Bazil... I'll do anything..." he whispered...

"Please understand..." Bazil said as he continued to cry... I know how much this hurts... it hurts me too... but it hurts Beautiee more than it hurts both of us... and I can't hurt her anymore...

"How will I make it without you?" Trevor cried.

"Find another man... quickly..." Bazil said as he wiped Trevor's tears...

"Damn... she really is the one isn't she?"

"Yes Trevor... she is..."

"I should've known this was coming... you married her right after you met her..."

"I fucked up Trevor..."

"You've fucked up before Bazil..."

"Yes I did... but Beautiee's different..."

"What makes her so damn special?" Trevor asked and then jumped back from Bazil... "I'm sorry... I didn't mean..."

"She came back Trevor..."

"Yea... you said things couldn't be better..."

"She told me she can't lose me..."

"Wait... What?"

"I fucked up... I brought you into the house... I told her everything... she knows how much I love you... she left me... I thought I lost her... but she came back to me... and told me she can't lose me... she chose me again Trevor..."

"What do you mean again?"

"She chose me when I asked her to marry me... she chose me when she turned to Sonia... and she chose me even after I told her I loved you... so... I'm choosing her..."

"Sonia? From the bank?"

"Yes Trevor..."

"Damn... I know you got good dick Baby... but..."

"That's not all there is to it Trevor," Bazil laughed.

"Say what you want Bazil... but you know you got good dick," Trevor laughed.

"That may be true... but my dick wasn't good enough to keep the others..."

"I'll miss you Bazil..."

"Find another man... quickly..."

"Will I ever see you again?"

"You'll see me from time to time... as I need you..."

"Okay Bazil... I guess this is goodbye," Trevor said as he pulled Bazil into a final kiss...

"Goodbye Trevor," Bazil said as he got up to leave, let himself out, and closed the door...

"Mutha fucka got some nerve thinking he's gonna dump me for that Bitch... I don't give a damn how good her pussy is... fuck this..." he said as he picked up his cell phone... "Hello? May I speak to Sonia please?"

"One moment please," the receptionist said as she transferred the call to Sonia's extension...

"Sonia speaking..."

"Meet me at Fridays..." Trevor said as he grabbed his jacket and his keys...

# Chapter 17

"Hey Trevor..." Sonia said as Trevor sat down...

"What the fuck Sonia!"

"Trevor please... I'm not in the mood..."

"You had one job to do Sonia... one job – and you couldn't even do that..."

"I tried!" Sonia cried.

"May I take your order?" Latasha asked.

"Henessey straight up... and whatever the lady wants," Trevor answered...

"Sex on the Beach... and make it strong..." Sonia said.

"I'll be right back," Latasha said as she went to get their drinks...

"I'm sorry Sonia... I don't mean to take it out on you... please don't cry..."

"I hate him Trevor... I swear... I hate him..."

"What happened Sonia?"

"Where do I start," she said as Latasha came back with their drinks...

"May I suggest some appetizers?"

"No thank you," Sonia answered.

"Okay... if you change your mind... I'll be over there," Latasha said as she pointed to her station...

"Bazil came to see me today..." she said as she started shaking...

"Sonia... Oh my God!" Trevor said as he got up, took his drink, and sat down beside Sonia. "Did he hurt you?"

"Yes... in a manner of speaking..." she whispered...

"Oh my God... what happened?"

"He came to see me... he started kissing me... he started touching me..."

"Oh God... please tell me he didn't..."

"No Trevor... he didn't hurt me like that... but he did hurt me..."

"I'm confused..."

"He invited me to his house..."

"Oh shit!"

"He wants me to make love to his wife... while he watches... and then he wants me to let him make love to me..."

"Damn!"

"He was so turned on by me making love to his wife... he put his hand between my legs..."

"Like this?" Trevor said as he slid his hand between Sonia's legs...

"Trevor... don't... please..."

"Ssshhhh... doesn't this feel good?" Trevor whispered in her ear as he slipped his hand inside her panties...

"Yes... but we're in public..."

"No one knows what's going on but us..." Trevor whispered as he slid two fingers inside Sonia...

"Trevor..." Sonia moaned...

"This is what you wanted from Bazil earlier... isn't it?" he breathed as he kissed her neck..."

"Yeessss..." Sonia moaned...

"What happened Sonia?" Trevor breathed as Sonia opened Trevor's pants and pulled his dick out under the table and started playing with it...

"He started fucking me with his fingers... oooohhh..." Sonia moaned...

"Like this?" Trevor asked as he drove his fingers in deeper..."

"Shit... Trevor... yeesss..."

"Did he make you cum?" he asked as he started massaging her G spot..."

"Nooo... ooohhh... Trevor..." Sonia moaned...

"Yes Sonia..." Trevor breathed as he continued to massage her G spot while she continued stroking his dick..."

"I'm cumming Trevor... please don't stop..." Sonia moaned a little louder...

"Ssshhhh... I won't stop..."

"Trevor... Trevor... Trevor... oh shit... that's it... yess... Trevor...."

"Yes Sonia..."

"I'm cummingg..." she moaned as quiet as she could...

"So am I... Sonia... Fuck!"

"Thank you Trevor... I needed that..." Sonia breathed. ..

"So did I Sonia..." Trevor breathed as he put the napkin in his lap, wiped his dick clean, and put the napkin back on the table... "So... what happened with you and Beautiee?"

"Everything..."

"So why is she going back to Bazil then?"

"I couldn't pull her..."

"Not even with The Extreme?"

"She wouldn't let me..."

"Let you? Since when do you give them a choice?"

"I had to go easy with her... she's different..."

"Oh shit! You got turned out! I thought I taught you better than that?"

"I know Trevor..." she said as she finished her drink... "but she fucked me so good..."

"Wait a minute... you mean to tell me... you let her fuck you... and you didn't return the favor?"

"She got me open Trevor... I let her do what she wanted to me... and I liked it... I asked her to fuck me... I was so turned on when she said yes... and then she fucked me better than I've been fucked in a long time..."

"Are you sure she's never done this before?"

"She said no..."

"Hmmmmm... I wonder..."

"I wish I could pull her away from Bazil... but she's so dickmatized by him when I suggested she let me try the dildo on her she got angry and jumped up off the bed... I had to work hard to get her to come back..."

"Come back?"

"Yes... she was at my house every night last week..."

"So... you had a whole week with her... and you still couldn't pull her away from Bazil?"

"I gave her multiples... and she still wouldn't let me fuck her..."

"Bazil came to see me today too..."

"What happened Trevor?"

"He said it's over..." Trevor answered with tears in his eyes...

"I'm sorry Trevor," Sonia said as she rubbed Trevor's hand...

"So am I... I love him soo much... but that's okay... he's going to pay for what he did to me... he's going to pay for what he did to both of us..."

# Chapter 18

"Hey Sonia," I said as I walked into the bank.

"Mrs. Osgood!" Mr. Cochran said when he saw me... "Nice to see you!"

"It's nice to see you too Mr. Cochran," I replied.

"Sonia?"I asked...

"Yes Mrs. Osgood?"

"May we speak in private?"

"Sure..." she said as we went into her office and closed the door... "How can I help you Mrs. Osgood," Sonia sighed as she sat down...

"What's wrong Sonia..."

"Nothing... its' just been one of those days," she sighed.

"Well... I said as I stepped closer to her... "I came here to ask you something..."

"Okay..." she said as I began massaging her shoulders...

"Please stop..."

"Okay..." I said as I moved away from her and sat down across from her...

"What do you need?"

"Right now I need for you to tell me why you're upset with me..." I said.

"I'm sorry Mrs. Osgood... its' just that I'm at work..."

"Okay... Well... I wanted to ask you something..."

"Yes Mrs. Osgood?"

"I told my husband about us..."

"Us? There is no us... you made that perfectly clear..."

"You're right... but I also said the door's open..."

"Are you saying you'd like to see me again?"

"I'm saying we'd like to see you..."

"Excuse me?"

"I told my husband about us... and told him how much I enjoyed being with you..."

"You enjoyed being with me?"

"Yes Sonia... I enjoyed being with you..."

"I enjoyed being with you too..." she said as she touched my hand... "But what's this got to do with your husband?"

"Well... he wants you to come to the house and make love to me... while he watches...

"Mrs. Osgood... I'm not sure that's a good idea..."

"Why not?"

"That can get very messy... and I don't do messy..."

"He just wants to watch..."

"He's a man with a dick... he'll watch... and then he'll want to join in..."

"I don't understand... you use a dildo..."

"Yes Mrs. Osgood - I use a dildo – because a dildo isn't attached to anyone or anything – there's no feelings involved – it does what I need it to do, then it goes back in the drawer – and it doesn't come back out until I need it again – and it will never, ever, control me..."

"Is that what you think my husband does to me?"

"That's what all men do Mrs. Osgood – that's why I have no desire to be with a man..."

"My husband's not controlling me..."

"Mrs. Osgood - you're here – asking me to have a threesome with you and your husband – because it's what your husband wants – if that's not control – then what is it?"

"Yes Sonia... my husband did ask me to invite you to our bedroom... but I'm here because I want to be..."

"So... you want me to have a threesome with you and your husband?"

"No Sonia..."

"Well then... what do you want?"

"Well... when my husband asked me if I enjoyed you... I told him I did. He asked me how many times you made me cum... so when he said he wanted to watch you make me cum... the thought of him watching turned me on..."

"Wow... you are something else Mrs. Osgood..."

"I'll take that as a compliment..." I laughed.

"I didn't really mean it that way..."

"So what do you mean?"

"I'm glad I turn you on... but do you really believe your husband just wants to watch?"

"No..."

"Okay then... so you understand why I don't think it's a good idea..."

"Yes... I understand..."

"It's better if we don't start something that could lead to nothing but problems..."

"I guess you're right..."

"Can I ask you something?"

"Sure..."

"If I said yes..."

"Okay..."

"What if your husband wanted to join in? How would you feel about that?"

"Well... honestly... since I slept with you... I guess I'd be okay with it..."

"So... you come here to ask me to have a threesome with you and your husband... and you're not sure how you feel about it?"

"Well... yea..."

"Let me ask you this... what if I fuck your husband... and I like it?"

"This is so easy when you're watching porn..." I sighed.

"Exactly – they don't show you what happens when the camera goes off. Did you know most porn stars are either single or married to another porn star?"

"No."

"Why do you think that is?"

"Because... I can't imagine going home to Bazil and saying not tonight honey... I've been fucking all day," I laughed.

"I just want you to understand what you're asking me..."

"I do..."

"There's something I need to tell you Mrs. Osgood..."

"Yes?"

"Please don't be upset..."

"Okay..."

"I enjoyed being with you... but I couldn't fuck your husband if I wanted to... and trust me... I don't want to..."

"Did something happen between you and my husband?"

"No Mrs. Osgood..."

"Oh thank God," I breathed."

"See? That's what I mean — you're relieved nothing happened between us — but you're here asking me to fuck him..."

"Sonia..."

"What?" she snapped.

"I'm not relieved nothing happened between you... I'm relieved he didn't hurt you..."

"Why would you think he'd hurt me?"

"I can see it in your face..."

"What you see is anger..."

"Because I went back to him?"

"Because he's just like my father – he uses women then tosses them when he's done with them unless they leave him first..."

"How do you know so much about my husband?"

"Forget it... I shouldn't have said anything..."

"It's a little late for that Sonia..." I said as I got up to leave...

"Beautiee... wait... please..." she said as she pulled me into a kiss...

"Have a good day Sonia..." I said as I opened the door, walked out her office, and out the bank.

# Chapter 19

"Beautiee..." Bazil said as he pulled me into a kiss...

"Hey my Thirst Quencher..." I sighed.

"What's wrong?"

"I'm just tired..." I lied.

"Beautiee..." he whispered in my ear as he began massaging my shoulders... "You're lying... please don't lie to me..." he said as he started kissing me on my neck...

"Mmmmmm... that feels nice..."

"Beautiee... tell me..."

"Okay..." I breathed as I turned around and pulled Bazil into a kiss...

"Mmmmmm... I know what you're up to..." Bazil moaned...

"I know what you're up to... too..." I moaned as I began massaging his dick through his pants...

"Come with me," Bazil commanded as he took me into the living room, laid down on the couch, and pulled me down on top of him... "Mmmmmm..." he moaned as I loosened his belt and released his dick from his pants...

"Mmmmmm..." I moaned as I lifted my skirt and slid down on his dick...

"Mmmmmph...          Mmmmmph... Mmmmmph..." Bazil moaned as I rode his dick...

"Bazil... Fuck!" I moaned as I pushed myself up with my hands and continued riding...

"Umph... Umph... Umph..." Bazil growled as he grabbed me by the waist and began thrusting...

"Bazil... I'm cummmmmmiiiinnnnggg.... I'm cummmmmmiiiinnnnggg...."

"Oh shit... fuuuuccckkkkk!" Bazil growled as I collapsed on top of him...

Bazil..." I breathed... "That was so fuckin' good..."

"Indeed..." Bazil breathed as he held me...

"I need to tell you something Bazil..."

"I know..."

"You do?"

"Yes Beautiee..."

"How did you know?"

"I saw it in your face..."

"Why didn't you stop me?"

"Because..." he said as he kissed me... "Your... face... is... beautiful... when... you... cum..."

"Oh Bazil... I love you..."

"I love you too..."

"I went to see Sonia today..."

"You did?"

"Yes Bazil..."

"What happened?"

"She doesn't think it's a good idea..."

"HhhMmmmmm... did she say why?"

"She gave me lots of reasons – she asked me if I would be okay if she fucked you... and liked it..."

"Would you?"

"To be honest... I don't know..."

"Is that why you were so upset?"

"No..."

"There's something else?"

"Yes..."

"Okay..."

"She said she couldn't fuck you if she wanted to because you're too much like her father..." I could feel Bazil tense up immediately...

"What else did she say?" he asked as he sat up a little...

"She said you use women and toss them aside when you're done with them... unless they leave you first..." Bazil was so angry his body got hard... "Did something happen between you and Sonia that you haven't told me?" I asked with tears in my eyes...

"Come here Beautiee..." he said as he sat up... "Sonia and I have known each other for a long time..."

"You have?"

"Yes Beautiee. When I first met Sonia she told me about her father... and she asked for my help..."

"So you helped her?"

"Yes Beautiee..."

"Did anything else ever happen between you?"

"Yes... and no..."

"What does that mean?"

"She needed a job so I spoke to Mr. Cochran on her behalf. We went out a few times – we kissed – we touched – but that's as far as it went..."

"Did you ever hurt her?" I asked with tears in my eyes, pleading for him to tell me he hadn't...

"Beautiee..."

"Yes Bazil?"

"I've never hurt Sonia... or any other woman..." he answered.

"She told me that..."

"She did?"

"Yes."

"So why was she so angry today?"

"Because... I went to see her..."

"You did?"

"Yes..."

"When?"

"After you told me what happened between you..."

"Were you angry?"

"No Beautiee... I was turned on when you told me what happened... remember?"

"Yes... I remember..."

"I went to invite her to come here... so I could watch..."

"Did she get angry?"

"Actually... she seemed open to the idea..."

"Well... after what happened today... she's closed..."

"Give her time... she'll calm down..."

"She said I was there because you were controlling me... with your dick..." I laughed.

"You know what? That's funny – especially because you left me to be with her – my dick had nothing to do with it," he laughed.

"I told her I was there because the thought of you watching me turned me on..."

"Don't worry about it Beautiee..."

"I'm not... not anymore..." I sighed as I snuggled up next to Bazil.

# Chapter 20

"Sonia... what are you doing here?" Trevor asked as he opened the door...

"I fucked up..." she said as she came in and sat down on the couch...

"Let me get you something to drink," Trevor sat as he went into the kitchen and came back with a glass... "Here... drink..." Trevor said as he sat down next to her...

"Thank you..." she breathed as she gulped it down fast...

"What happened?"

"First Bazil... now Beautiee..."

"What happened?"

"She came to see me... to ask me to come to the house and make love to her – while he watches!"

"Well... don't you like Beautiee?"

"I love her..."

"Sonia!"

"She's not the problem... it's that no good mutha fuckin' husband of hers..."

"So... what's wrong with that?"

"Everything! I can't stand him! He says he just wants to watch but he'll join in! I don't want him anywhere near me!"

"Really?"

"What's that supposed to mean?"

"You didn't have a problem with him being near you the other day..."

"Fuck you Trevor!"

"If you insist..." he said as he leaned in to kiss her...

"I can't with you men! Uuuggghhh!"

"Sonia! What the hell's a matter with you?"

"Bazil's been trying to fuck me for years..."

"Oh... I get it..."

"I swear... I wish I never touched Beautiee..."

"I thought you love her?"

"I do... but I told her I couldn't fuck her husband if I wanted to – I told her he was manipulating her with his dick – I told her he uses women and tosses them aside when he's done with them – I told her..."

"Sonia!"

"What!"

"Come here..." Trevor said as he pulled her close and held her...

"She's gonna run and tell Bazil everything I said," she cried.

"So what?"

"So what? You know what'll happen Trevor...

"Sonia... he's not going to hurt you..."

159

"How can you be so sure?"

"If he wanted to hurt you... he would've done that already..."

"I just wish he'd go the fuck away... and stay away..."

"Shhh... it'll be alright Sonia..." Trevor whispered as he kissed her softly."

"Thank you..."

"For what?"

"For letting me vent..."

"I think you should do it..."

"Trevor!"

"Hear me out..."

"Aaiight... go 'head..."

"Call Beautiee... tell her you've had a change of heart..."

"I don't want to Trevor..."

"You just leave the door unlocked... so I can let myself in... I'll come upstairs... I'll wait 'till just the right moment... and I'll take care of him for good..."

"Trevor! Are you serious?"

"Yes Sonia..."

"You'll get caught..."

"No I won't..."

"How can you be sure?"

"I've been there before... I know where to slip out..."

"I don't want Bazil anywhere near me..."

"Sonia... think about this... you'd have Beautiee all to yourself..."

"How?"

"Beautiee will grieve... she'll need to turn to someone... and you'll be there to help her get through it..."

"HMmmmm... you have a point there..."

"Now that's more like it..." Trevor said as he kissed her again...

"Trevor... stop..."

"Why..."

"I didn't come here for this..."

"Haven't you ever thought about it?"

"Yes..."

"Well..."

"I'm not ready Trevor..."

"Sonia... you're a beautiful woman..."

"You've only been with one woman..."

"You've never been with a man..."

"No I haven't..."

"We could be there for each other..."

"Can I trust you?"

"Yes Sonia... you can trust me..." he breathed as he began massaging her breasts..."

"That feels nice Trevor..." she moaned...

"Come with me..." Trevor said as he stood up, extended his hand to take hers, and walked her to the bedroom...

"Trevor..." she moaned as he kissed her neck and shoulders... "I don't think I can do this..."

"I'm not Bazil..." he said as he began unbuttoning her blouse..."

"I know..." she whispered as she kissed him back...

"Let me take off your clothes..." he said as he stood in front of her, slipped off her blouse, her bra, her skirt, her panties, and stood back to admire her. "Sonia... my God... you're so beautiful..." he breathed as he pulled her close to him, held her, and kissed her...

"Let me help you out of your clothes..." she said as she pulled his shirt over his head. Trevor stood still and allowed her to loosen his belt and slide his pants and boxers off his ass, taking her time to feel his ass as she did so... "Oh my God!" Sonia whispered... "You're dick is... May I?" she asked as she stepped towards Trevor and began stroking his dick...

"Yeeessss....." Trevor moaned as he stood there, watching her stroke him...

"Oooohhhh..." Sonia gasped when Trevor pulled her close to him and held her naked body against his...

"Sonia..." he breathed as she backed away from him towards the bed and lay down on her back. Trevor went over to the bed, laid down beside Sonia, and began rubbing his hand up and down her body as he leaned in to kiss her. Sonia pulled him on top of her, spreading her legs and bending them slightly, giving Trevor access... "Sonia..." Trevor breathed as he inserted himself inside her and began thrusting slowly...

"Oh Trevor..." Sonia moaned as she held on to him and began meeting his thrusts. Trevor continued to take his time, alternating between kissing her neck, her breasts, and her mouth.

Sonia began to moan softly as she grabbed Trevor's ass and push him deeper inside her... "Trevor... Trevor... Trevor..." Trevor, taking his cue from Sonia, began thrusting harder...

"Sonia... Sonia... Sonia..."

"I'm cumming Trevor... please don't stop..."

"I won't Sonia... I won't..."

"Oh yes... that's it... Trrreeeevvvvooooorrrr!"

"Sonia! Sonia! Sonia! Uuugggggghhhh!"

"Trevor... that... was..." Sonia started to say until she burst into tears...

"Sonia..." Trevor said as he pulled her close and held her...

"Thank you..."

"My pleasure..." Trevor smiled as he continued to hold Sonia and kiss her...

"I never wanted Bazil..." she whispered.

"I know..." Trevor said as he kissed her again... "I know..."

"I'll do it..."

"You will?"

"Yes..."

"Good..."

"Promise me you'll be there..."

"I will... I promise..."

# Chapter 21

"Hello Sonia..." I said loud enough for Bazil to hear as I answered my cell...

"Hey Beautiee..." Sonia said as I put the phone on speaker... "I just wanted to call and apologize for what happened earlier...

"You don't need to apologize Sonia..."

"Yes Beautiee... I do..."

"I'm sorry I made you uncomfortable..."

"I was just taken aback..."

"I understand Sonia..."

"Let me explain Beautiee..."

"Okay..."

"I've never been with a married woman before..."

"Ooohhh..."

"Before you, I was only with single women... no strings... sometimes they wanted a relationship... sometimes they wanted sex... sometimes they wanted others... but it was always just between us..."

"Uh huh..."

"Then you came along... I knew you were married... I never should have suggested anything in the first place... but you were in bad shape and I wanted... needed... to comfort you..."

"Oh Sonia! How Sweet!" I exclaimed as Bazil's face lit up...

"Once you kissed me... which I never expected... I was done..."

"I didn't plan that... it just happened..."

"I could tell it was genuine... you're so sweet..."

"Aawwww... thank you Sonia..." I said as Bazil pulled me closer...

"I fell in love with you Beautiee... I know I shouldn't have... but I couldn't help it..." she said to Bazil's delight...

"I'm sorry if I led you on Sonia... I didn't mean to..."

"I know you didn't Beautiee..."

"I care about you... but I love Bazil..."

"As you should... he's your husband... that's why when you invited me to your home I freaked out... I can't be the other woman in your marriage..."

"I'm sorry Sonia... I never meant to make you feel that way..."

"I know you didn't Beautiee... how could you know... you've never done anything like this before..."

"It looks so easy in porn..."

"As I said – they're actors – and they never show you what happens when the cameras go off..."

"Well... you did ask me if you'd ever see me again..."

"Yes I did..."

"And I told you the door was open..."

"Yes you did..."

"So... when someone opens the door for you... isn't it rude not to come in?"

"Beautiee... I can't with you..." she laughed.

"I understand how you feel Sonia... it's just that I've always fantasized about..."

"About what Beautiee?" Sonia asked as Bazil looked at me perplexed, waiting for me to answer...

"I've always fantasized about being with a woman... and getting caught by my husband... and him joining in..." I answered as Bazil beamed...

"Oh wow... I had no idea..."

"I've never told anyone that before..."

"I feel honored you shared that with me..."

"I've never been with a woman before and since I've been with you... as you said... I've broadened my horizon... and my orgasms..."

"Awww... Damn Beautiee... you about to make me cry..."

"I'll tell you something else Sonia..."

"What's that?"

"Bazil says since I've been with you... I taste sweeter..."

"Okay Beautiee... okay... enough already... I'll do it... just once..."

"You will?"

"Yes Beautiee... I'll do it... but I do have two conditions..."

"Yes Sonia?"

"Number one... your husband can watch... but if he joins in, he's not to touch me..."

"Okay..."

"Number two... I'm expecting that you will make love to me as well..."

"I'm looking forward to it Sonia..."

"Are you?"

"Yeeesss..."

"Okay Beautiee... how's Friday night at 8:00 p.m.?"

"Perfect..." I said as Bazil kissed me...

"Do I need to bring anything?"

"No Sonia..."

"Okay... I'll see you both Friday night..."

"Sonia..." Trevor breathed as he answered the phone...

"We're all set for Friday night at 8:00 p.m."

"You sure Beautiee doesn't suspect anything?"

"Hell no... she told me she's always fantasized about being with another woman... and getting caught by her husband... and him joining in..."

"Oh shit!"

"She wants to indulge in her fantasy with me!" Sonia beamed.

"Damn Sonia... I wish I could join in too..."

"I told her I had two conditions..."

"Oh yea?"

"Yea – number one – her husband doesn't touch me..."

"What'd number two?"

"I expect her to make love to me too..."

"Damn Sonia... I can't wait to see this..."

"Don't let me down Trevor..."

"I won't Sonia... I'll see you Friday night..."

# Chapter 22

"Come in Sonia..." I said as I opened the door...

"Hi Beautiee..." Sonia said as she came in and closed the door behind her... leaving it slightly cracked...

"Come with me..." I said as I took her by the hand and walker her into the kitchen...

"Your home is lovely..."

"Thank you..." I said as I shooed Bazil away from the doorway, opened the wine, and poured two glasses... "Moscato?"

" Yes... thank you..." she said as we both started drinking...

"Sonia... I'm nervous as hell..." I whispered...

"Oh thank God..." she laughed... "I thought it was just me..."

"I remember you gave me wine on our first night together..." I said as I went towards her...

"Yes... I did..." she said as she pulled me into a kiss...

"Mmmmmm...." I moaned as she slipped her tongue in my mouth. I could see Bazil watching us from the corner of my eye and it turned me on. We finished our wine, put our glasses down on the island, and continued kissing each other for a few minutes until I spoke... "C'mon Sonia... let's go upstairs..."

"Okay..." she said as she followed me upstairs, down the hall, and into our bedroom... "Oh wow... you have a lovely suite..."

"Thank you..."

"So... shall I sit?" she asked as she patted the bed...

"Please..." I said as I sat down beside her... "I can't believe I'm doing this..." I whispered...

"Hmmmmm... neither can I..." she said as she began unbuttoning my blouse. I unbuttoned Sonia's blouse and we both slid our blouses off each other's shoulders at the same time. Neither of us was wearing a bra so we both began massaging each other's breasts and started kissing. I saw Bazil watching us, fully naked, from the closet, while he was stroking his dick... and I wanted it...

"Lay down on your back..." I commanded. Sonia lay down and I slid her pants down off of her and tossed them to the floor. I slid my own pants off, tossed them to the floor, and lay between her legs...

"Beautiee...." She moaned as I started sucking her breasts. I started kissing Sonia down her body and continued kissing until I reached her pussy. I put my face down and put my ass up, knowing what Bazil was going to do...

"Ooohhh…" I moaned as Bazil grabbed me by the waist and started fucking me from behind…

"Beautiee… yeeesss….." Sonia moaned as my tongue went up inside her pussy…

"Yeesss…" Bazil moaned as he thrust harder…

"Mmmmmm…." I moaned in Sonia's pussy, licking and sucking with each thrust…

"Make her cum…" Bazil commanded as he fucked me harder…

"Mmmmmm…. MmmmMmmm…. MmmmMmmm….." I moaned into Sonia's pussy as she began riding my face…

"Beautiee… Beautiee… don't stop… don't stop…

"Your pussy is so fuckin' wet…" Bazil growled… Ugggh! Ugggh! Ugggh!"

"Mmmmmm…. Mmmmmm…. Mmmmmm…." I moaned in Sonia's pussy as she grabbed my head…

"Oh shit… fuck… I'm cumming!" Sonia screamed as she clamped her legs around my head and rode my face harder. Bazil was so turned on he took it out on my pussy and my legs began shaking uncontrollably…

"Mmmmmm! Mmmmmm! Mmmmmm! I moaned into Sonia's pussy as her orgasmic wave was coming down her body while my orgasmic wave was going up my body and we both collapsed on top of Sonia…

"UMmmmm... I can't breathe..." Sonia laughed...

"Sorry about that..." Bazil said as he got up off me and stood there looking down at us...

"Are you ready?" Sonia breathed as I kissed her...

"Yes... I'm... ready..." I said in between kisses...

"I really enjoyed that..." Sonia breathed...

"So did I..." Bazil breathed. I could feel Sonia tensing up as she heard Bazil's voice so I tried to make her comfortable...

"I'm glad you enjoyed me Sonia..." I breathed as I kissed her again and she rolled me over on my back.

"Open your legs..." Sonia commanded as she started sucking my breasts...

"Mmmmmm..." I moaned as she kissed her way down my stomach to my pussy...

"Bazil..." I moaned as she started licking, slurping, and sucking. I looked at Bazil and saw how turned on he was... so much so that he started stroking his dick again... "Oh Bazil..." I moaned as she put her tongue inside my pussy, licking, sucking, and slurping from inside, out, and inside again... "Bazil... she's gonna make me cum..." I moaned...

"Mmmmmm..." Bazil moaned as he came over and put his dick in my mouth...

"Mmmmmm..... Mmmmmm..... Mmmmmm....." I moaned on Bazil's dick as Sonia put her hands up under me, lifted my ass up off the bed, and dove in... "Baaazzziiilll! Look out!" I screamed as I saw the gun... but it was too late...

"Aagggggghhhh!" Bazil cried out as he tried to dodge the bullet... but failed...

"Sonia!" I grabbed her up from between my legs and held her down on my body to shield us both but realized what was going on when she got hit...

"Sonia! Nooooo!" Trevor cried as he dropped the gun to rush to her... "This is all your fault Beautiee! She didn't deserve to die!" he cried...

"She deserved to die... and so do you!" I screamed as I grabbed the gun before Trevor could... and pulled the trigger...

"Beautiee! Beautiee! It's Keisha... you okay in there?"

"Oh God... Baaazzziiillll!" I screamed as I dropped the gun on the floor...

"Keisha... what's wrong?" her husband Troy asked as he ran towards our house...

"She needs help... break the door..."

"The police are on their way Keisha – let's go!"

"Mutha fucka I said break the fuckin' door... NNNOOOOWWWW!!!"

"Fine – but I ain't payin' for this shit!" he growled as he broke the door down and they came rushing upstairs...

"Beautiee! Where are you?" Troy yelled...

"I'm in here!" I screamed...

173

"Oh Shit! What the fuck... Yo Keisha... we out..."

"Please don't leave me!" I cried...

"Troy – get a robe!" Keisha said as she tried to shield me from her husband...

"Here..." Troy said as he tossed the robe to Keisha...

"Here Beautiee... put this on..." she said as she helped me put on the robe...

"Damn Keisha... you got blood all over your clothes..." Troy said as he shook his head...

"I don't give a fuck about these clothes!" Keisha yelled...

"Oh shit - the cops are here – yo Keisha – lets go!"

"I'm not leaving her Troy – look at her! Damn... I'm sorry Beautiee... are you okay?"

"Bazil... I whispered as I pointed towards Bazil..."

"Is he dead?" Troy asked...

"Step aside sir," the techs from the ambulance said as they pushed their way into the room...

"Bazil..." I said as I pointed towards Bazil...

"We've got a pulse - he's still alive – let's get him to the hospital – stat!" they said as I watched them lift Bazil's bloody unconscious body onto the stretcher...

"Bazil!" I screamed as I ran down the stairs behind them, not bothering to close my robe...

"Maam... are you okay?" one of the techs asked...

"Bazil!" I screamed as I ran out the house following the stretcher... and ran right into Katina Jones...

"Mrs. Osgood – oh my God – what happened?"

"Bazil!" I screamed as I pushed her down and the ambulance closed the door...

"Wait!" the driver said as he saw me running naked... covered in blood... robe swirling behind me...

"Is this your husband maam?" I didn't answer... I just snatched the door open and climbed in... and Keisha was right behind me...

"What the fuck happened here?" Katina asked as she went through the house, upstairs, and into the bedroom following the blood...

"Don't you fuckin' move!" Katina commanded as she drew her gun on Troy...

"Hold up – this some bullshit – I ain't have nothin' to do with this shit – all I did was break the door..."

"Oh shit – we got bodies!" she said as she got on her radio... "So... you said you broke down the door... why?"

"Because my wife told me to break the fuckin' door!"

"Do you always listen to your wife?"

"Yo – what the fuck is wrong with you asking me some shit like that – I'm out!" Troy said as he tried to leave..."

'I'm afraid I can't let you leave sir," Katina said as she stood in the doorway..."

"You better stand there all night then – 'cause as soon as you step aside – I'm out!"

"Detective Jones?"

"Yes Sergeant?"

"There's a gun on the floor over there," he said as he pointed towards the gun on the floor...

"Oh shit – guys – bag that..." she said as she turned to watch the officers... giving Troy the perfect opportunity to slip out...

"Get back here!" Katina yelled as Troy made it downstairs and slipped out the front door...

"Detective – we'll speak to him later – what the fuck happened here?" the Sergeant asked as the officers began processing the crime scene...

"Bazil Osgood is still breathing... these two are not..."

"Bazil Osgood? Hhhmmmmmmmmm..."

"His wife pushed me down to run get in the ambulance with her husband..."

"Did you get a chance to question her?"

"No I didn't – she's no good to me right now anyway..."

"What makes you say that?" he asked as the officers continued processing the crime scene...

"She ran past me... naked, covered in blood, wearing nothing but a robe..."

"We got a gunshot!" The paramedics yelled as they rushed in through the ambulance entrance...

"What happened?" a nurse tried to ask me but I followed behind the ambulance techs with Bazil...

"Excuse me Miss, can we get some information from you?" the nurse asked Keisha...

"Bazil Osgood – and that's his wife," Keisha answered as she ran behind me...

"What do we have here?" the doctor asked as he came running out...

"He's been shot... he's stabilized but we can't stop the bleeding..."

"Get him into surgery – stat – and get me Nurse Trinity..." the doctor said as he flew down the hall...

"Mrs. Osgood?"

"Yes?"

"We need you to wait here..." Nurse Trinity said...

"That's my husband!" I screamed as Keisha pulled me into a hug to console me...

"Mrs. Osgood - we need to get your husband into surgery - Dr. Preston's the best - We'll do everything we can!" she said as she rushed off behind Dr. Preston...

"Beautiee... sit down..." Keisha said she held me...

"Okay..." I cried...

"He's gonna make it..." she said reassuringly as she rubbed my hand...

"Mrs. Osgood?" another nurse said as she came up to me...

"Yes?" I answered as I looked up at her...

"Ummmmm..."

"Yes... Yvonne?" I asked as I read her name tag...

"You're naked... and you're both covered in blood...

"Yea..." I said as I stared off into space..."

"Maam?" Nurse Yvonne asked Keisha...

"Yes Nurse?"

"Are you hurt?"

"No," Keisha answered as her husband came running down the hall...

"Keisha!" Troy yelled when he saw her...

"I'm alright Troy," she said as he sat down...

"Mrs. Osgood?"

"Yes Nurse?"

"Can you come with me please?"

"I need to be here when my husband gets out of surgery..."

"Mrs. Osgood... I need you to come with me... please..."

"Why?"

"You're naked... you're covered in blood..."

"You want me to take a shower?" I laughed hysterically...

"I can't let you do that..."

"Excuse me?"

"Mrs. Osgood... your husband was shot... you were on the scene... we need to do a rape kit and get some samples..."

"Keisha... is she for real right now?" I laughed.

"Hell you askin' me for — I'on know!" Keisha laughed.

"My husband didn't rape me!" I snapped...

"Did anyone else rape you?"

"Hell no!"

"Umm... well... Mrs. Osgood... I don't understand... I'm new here... just come with me... please..."

"Okay..." I said as I followed Nurse Yvonne...

"Yo Keisha! That detective tried to get at me!" Troy said.

"Which detective?"

"I'on know the bitch name — I was out!"

"You should've ran after me," Keisha said.

"I didn't know you left! What the fuck happened?"

"I'on know! I heard Beautiee screamin' n' shit — that's why I told you to kick in the fuckin' door!"

"So that's what happened?" Katina Jones asked as she walked into the hallway...

"Who you talkin' to?" Keisha asked as she stood up...

"I'm talking to both of you... if that's alright..." Katina said as she sat down beside Keisha and Troy... "I want to apologize for what happened earlier," she said as she turned to Troy... "I came into the room, I saw bodies, I saw blood, and you were standing there..."

"It's cool – on some real shit though – I'on know what the fuck you were goin' do!" Troy laughed.

"Can you tell me what happened?" Katina asked...

"My wife told me to kick the door in – so I did – then we ran upstairs," Troy answered.

"Is this true?" Katina asked Keisha...

"Don't call my husband a liar!" Keisha snapped.

"I'm not – I just need you to corroborate his statement..."

"You right – I'm sorry – I heard Beautiee screaming so I ran over to the house...

"You live next door?" Katina interrupted...

"Yea..."

"Okay – go ahead..."

"So my husband asked me what was going on – I told him I heard screaming and told him to break the fuckin' door down so he did – we ran upstairs..."

"What happened after you got upstairs?"

"Beautiee was naked... Bazil was naked... somebody else was naked... there was blood everywhere... I went to Beautiee to hold her... my husband got her a robe..."

"Is that her blood on you?"

"I'on know whose blood this is..." Keisha answered.

"I'm gonna need to bag your clothes as evidence..."

"Troy – can you go home and get me some clothes?"

"Aaiight – I'll be back..." Troy said as he left...

"This is Nurse Tisha," Nurse Yvonne explained as I was escorted into another examining room...

"Mrs. Osgood?" Nurse Tisha asked...

"Yes?"

"We need to take some pictures... get some samples... and do a rape kit..." she said as she patted the table for me to sit...

"I wasn't raped..." I said...

"We still need to do a rape kit..."

"You can take your pictures – you can get your samples – but you're not doing a rape kit," I said as I dropped my robe...

"Oh my God – what happened?" she asked as she got the camera and began taking pictures...

"My husband got shot," I answered...

"Did you shoot him?"

"You know what – hurry up with your pictures and your swabs so I can get back to my husband!" I snapped.

"I'm sorry... it's just... never mind..."

"It's just you thought I was an angry woman that caught her husband cheating... and shot his ass," I laughed...

"Yea..." she laughed as she put the camera down and began swabbing me... "Lift you neck so I can get some swabs there..."

"Okay..."

"You're all set Mrs. Osgood..."

"Thank you Tisha..." I said as I put the robe back on and headed back towards the waiting area...

"Shit... almost got it... got it!" Dr. Preston said as he held up the bullet before dropping it in the dish...

"Okay... let's get him closed up," Dr. Preston sighed...

"Doctor..." Nurse Trinity said as she pointed to the monitor...

"Oh shit – he's coding!" Dr. Preston said as he grabbed the defibulator... "On three – one... two... three!"

"He's back doctor..."

"Okay – his pressure's dropping – Mr. Osgood – I need you to stop fighting for a sec – I'm trying to get you back to your wife – I can't do that if I can't close you up – shit – Nurse?"

"Yes Doctor?"

"His pressure is dropping again – come hold this open so I can get this clamp on..."

"Got it... doctor..."

"Okay Mr. Osgood... hang on... almost there... got it! Thanks Trinity – Mr. Osgood – I'm trying to get you back to your wife – I'm on your side here – I need you to relax okay?"

"You think he can hear you doctor?"

"My mother was in a comma last year – she told me she heard everything so... who knows," he said as he closed Bazil up... "Okay Mr. Osgood – Nurse Trinity is going to wash you up, dress you up, and get you back to your wife – thanks for cooperating..." he said as he turned to remove his gloves...

"Doctor – we have a problem..."

"Shit!"

# Chapter 23

"Mrs. Osgood..." Dr. Preston breathed when he saw me..."

"Yes Doctor Preston?" I asked, dreading what he was about to say...

"Your husband made it through surgery..."

"Oh thank God!" I cried as Keisha and Troy smiled...

"Mrs. Osgood..."

"What's wrong Doctor?" I asked...

"The surgery went okay but it took longer than expected..."

"Okay..."

"We had to keep stopping to stabilize him..."

"Okay..."

"His blood pressure keeps dropping..."

"Okay..."

"We had to put him in a medical comma..."

"You had to put him in a comma? I don't understand..." I said as I teared up...

"Your husband's body was fighting to get back but he lost a lot of blood and his pressure was too low – he's too weak right now to heal... if we didn't put him in a comma he might have slipped into one anyway – and he may not have come back..."

"Is my husband going to die?"

"Honestly... I don't know Mrs. Osgood..."

"What happens now?" I asked as I sat down and started crying...

"Do you believe in God?"

"Yes I do..."

"Then pray..." he said as he turned and walked towards the nurse's station...

"He's gonna be alright..." Keisha said as she rubbed my hand...

"Yes... he'll be fine..." I said as I stared off...

"Keisha... you need something to eat?" Troy asked...

"Yea – I am hungry... Beautiee... you want anything?"

"Sure... hold on a minute..." I said as I got up to go towards the nurse's station...

"Mrs. Osgood?"

"Yes Doctor Preston?"

"I gotta ask – why are you naked?" Keisha and Troy stood there with a 'No this Mutha Fucka Didn't Just Ask Her That' look on their faces...

"We were having sex..."

"You were having sex?"

"Yes..."

"I wanna make sure I'm understanding you correctly...

"Okay..."

"You were having sex when you're husband got shot?"

"Yea..."

"Is that your husband's blood on you?"

"Some of it is..."

"Oh my God – what the hell happened?"

"Long story..." I sighed.

"Do you have any clothes?"

"No..."

"So you threw on a robe, jumped in the ambulance, and came straight here – naked?"

"Yea..."

"Why didn't anyone get you any clothes?"

"There wasn't any time..."

"Are they done with you?"

"Yes..."

"Trinity! Get Mrs. Osgood a pair of pajamas ˉ and a shower!" he said as he started to walk away...

"Doctor Preston?"

"Yes Mrs. Osgood?"

"Can I stay?"

"You husbands in a medically induced comma – he isn't waking up anytime soon – go home – get some rest – then come back – we'll call you if anything changes..."

"Okay Doctor Preston..."

"C'mon Mrs. Osgood – let's get you in the shower and into some pajamas..."

"Keisha.... Wait for me please?" I could see Troy telling her hell no but Keisha paid him no mind...

"Okay Beautiee... but hurry up..."

"Okay... Love you..." I sang as I followed Nurse Trinity down the hall...

"Dammit Keisha! You should'a said no!" Troy snapped.

"She would do the same thing for me..." Keisha said...

"I ain't tryin' to be here all night Keisha..."

"You won't Baby... I promise..." Keisha said as she kissed him..."

"You lucky I love you..." he said as he kissed her back...

"I know that's right..." she said as she kissed him again...

"Ready..." I said as I came down the hall towards them...

"Those are some cute pajamas," Troy laughed.

"Thanks Troy..." I said as I kissed him on the cheek...

"Okay – where we goin?" Keisha asked...

"Cracker Barrel..." I answered.

"I was talkin' to Troy..." Keisha laughed...

"Cracker Barrel," Troy laughed as we all walked out the hospital together and I got in their car.

"Mommy... look!" the little boy laughed as we entered Cracker Barrel...

"Shhh... that's not polite," his mother corrected...

'But Mommy – she's wearing pajamas," the little boy laughed.

"Stop laughing at her!" His mother corrected...

"Excuse me... Miss?" the little boy asked as he tugged at my pajama top...

"Yes?" I answered...

"Why are you wearing pajamas?"

"Tommy! Get over here... I'm sorry Miss," his mother said as she snatched him away from me...

"That's okay..." I said to his mother... "I'm wearing pajamas because I just got out of the hospital," I explained to Tommy.

"What happened to your clothes?"

"They got really dirty so I had to leave them there," I explained...

"Ohhh... are they gonna get washed?"

"Yea..."

"Ohhh... that's nice... bye..." he said as his mother pushed him towards their table to be seated.  After we were seated, the waitress came to the table to take our orders:

"Welcome to Cracker Barrel – what can I get for you this evening?"

"Just give us one of everything on the dinner menu except pork," I answered.

"Excuse me?"

"Just give us one of everything on the dinner menu except pork!" I repeated.

"Miss... that's a lot of food... and we'll be closing soon... if you had been here about an hour earlier..."

"Just bring us one of everything you have – whatever you don't have - don't worry about it," I interrupted.

"Okay..." she said as she walked away...

"Who's eating all that food?" Keisha asked.

"We are," I said.

"We are?" Troy asked.

"You said you were hungry right?" I asked.

"Yea... but that's a lot of food," Keisha said.

"Whatever we don't eat, y'all can take home – my treat."

"Beautiee... you know this bill gonna be over $200 right?" Keisha asked.

"Here's a few of the dishes – as I said, we're about to close soon so I don't have everything..." the waitress said as she started placing the following food on the table – roast beef with mashed potatoes green beans, and carrots – country fried steak with corn – meatloaf with macaroni and cheese – parmesan crusted biscuit pot pie – country fried shrimp with fries – and farm raised catfish.

"I'll take the meatloaf and the shrimp!" I said before Keisha and Troy could say anything...

"I'm taking that country fried steak!" Troy said... "Keisha you can have all that," he laughed.

"I'm gonna tear that roast beef down... but you gonna help me eat some of this fish..." she said as she started eating...

"I'ma tear down that biscuit pot pie too," Troy said as we all continued eating...

"Thank you Lord for Keisha, Troy, and this food — AMEN!" I yelled as we all bust the food down.

"How was everything?" the waitress asked as she came over with glasses of water...

"Everything was soooooo goooooddd..." I breathed as I pulled out a $100 and slipped it in her pocket...

"Thank you miss," she said as she left the check on the table.

"Thank you Beautiee..." Troy said as we dragged ourselves away from the table...

"Thank you too..." I yawned. We all got in the car and sat quiet. We were too full to speak. When we pulled up to the house, I was afraid to get out the car... "I can't go in there..."

"You want me to go in with you?" Keisha asked.

"Keisha... let her go in there by herself..." Troy said as I started to cry... "Beautiee... we'll be right next door if you need us... but you need to do this..." Troy said as he put his arm around me...

"Okay..." I said as I walked up to the front door. When I saw the crime tape, I pulled it away from the door, went inside, and broke down crying. I cried for a while and then I remembered

I had wine in the kitchen... "What the hell is this?" I said as I saw a handwritten note under the bottle of Moscato:

Beautiee,

We knew you wouldn't be able to handle seeing the house after everything that happened so while you were at the hospital with Keisha I called the Merry Maids and had them clean the house for you.

You're welcome.

Troy

"I love y'all..." I said as I took a glass of Moscato and went upstairs. "Ooohhhhh wow.... I said when I saw how clean everything was. "You can't even tell anything happened here..." I whispered as I walked over to where Bazil was shot... "Bazil...." I whispered as I lay down on the bed and cried myself to sleep.

"Detective – I need you to take a look at this," the Coroner said as Katina walked over to Sonia and Trevor's dead bodies. "This is the bullet we removed from Bazil, this is the bullet we removed from Sonia, and this is the bullet we removed from Trevor."

"They're all the same," Katina said.

"Yes they are – and they all were shot from the gun you found on the scene..."

"I kinda figured that..." Katina said...

"There's more..."

"Okay – what is it?" Katina asked...

"We have two sets of finger prints on the gun used to kill them..."

"Two?" Katina asked.

"Yes."

"There were four people in that room – two are dead..." Katina said.

"Exactly – and Bazil's fingerprints aren't one of the two."

"Well Sonia didn't shoot herself... so that leaves..." Katina stopped and put her hand over her mouth...

"Beautiee and Trevor..." the coroner said as Katina flew out the door...

## <u>Twisted Beautiee Tree</u>

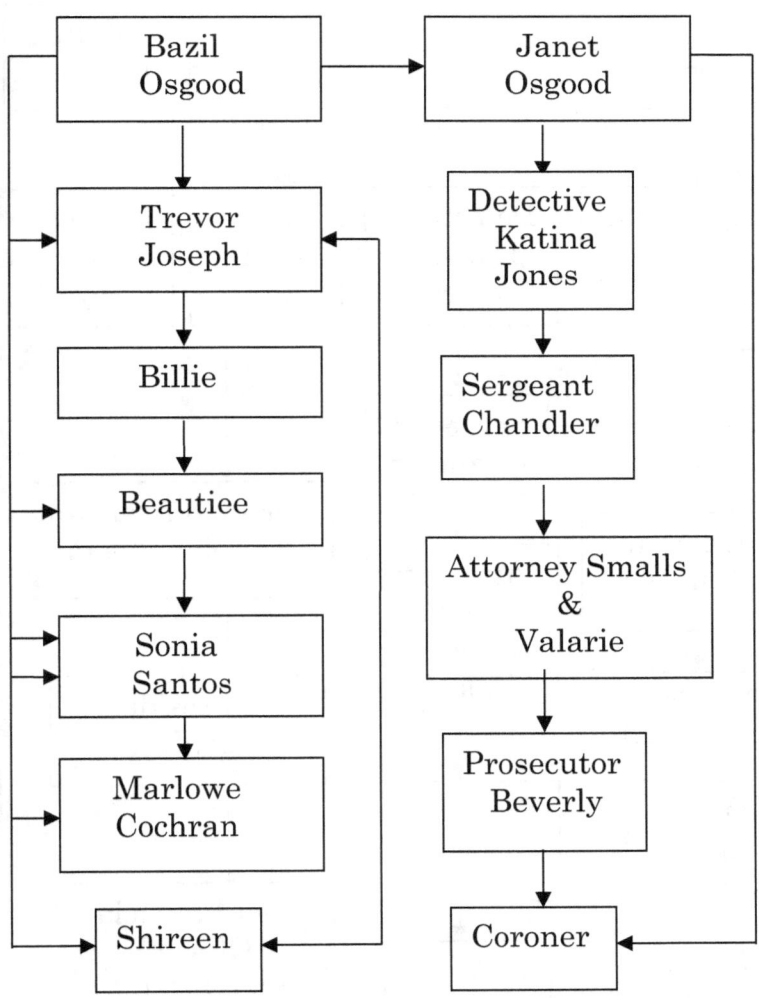

# Twisted Beautiee Tree

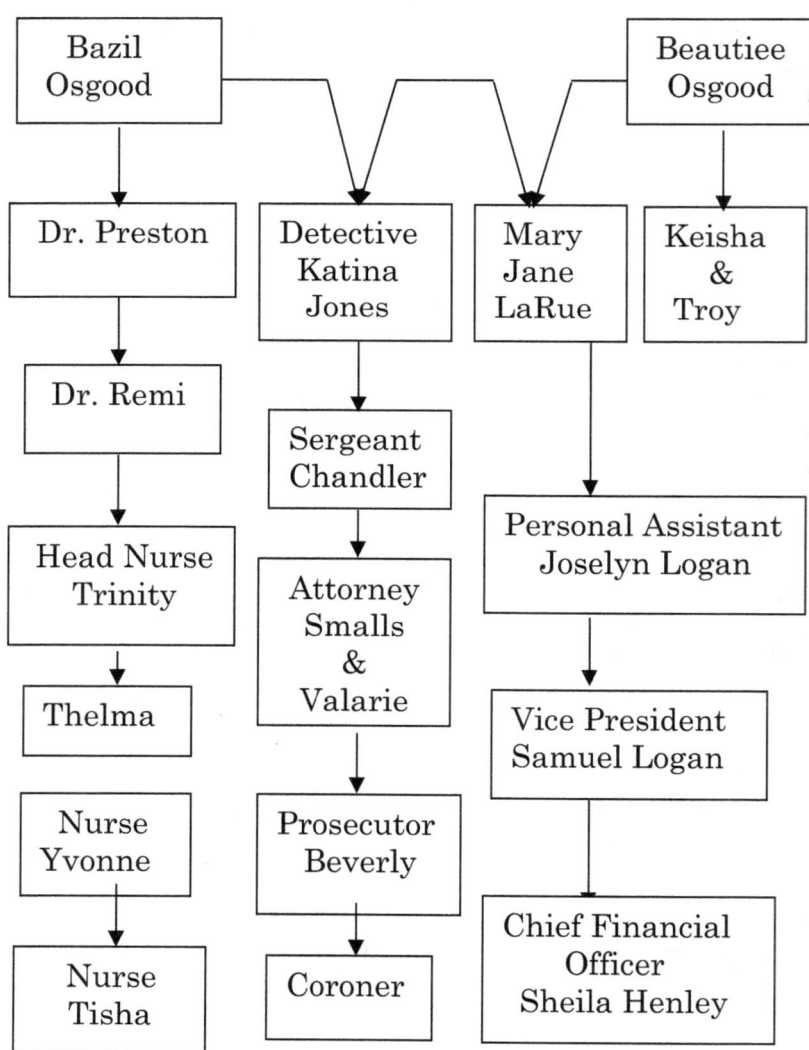